EDUCATING SARAH

by

Sophie Meredith

———

Golden Valley Publications

CHAPTER ONE

Sarah adjusted the hump of pillows in her bed, then pulled the

covers over the convincing body-like form. She pulled a thick, shapeless sweater over her outfit of faded shirt and fashionably disreputable jeans. Then she crept quietly down the stairs, through the dark, silent hall and out into the night.

Paula stirred in her sleep, fought her way back into the warm security of her dream, lost the battle, awoke. Uncertain what had disturbed her, she turned on the bedside lamp to look at her alarm clock. Midnight. The witching hour. She raised her head and listened to the barely-perceptible creaks and sighs of the old cottage. She sat up and reached for her kimono. She tiptoed to the door of the other bedroom and opened it just enough to make out the motionless figure in the bed. Her eyes were drawn then to the wardrobe, on the outside of which hung a magnificent creation in white lace, caught now in a beam of moonlight - her daughter's wedding dress. Paula's face was calm, even a little austere, but from the corner of her eye, unbidden, oozed a single tear. She left the door ajar and returned to her bed. Soon she was back in the familiar dream.

Sarah emerged from the lane on to the main road and broke into a run. Ahead blazed the lights of the café. Three lorries and several motorcycles were strewn around the forecourt. Sarah peered into a wing-mirror at her unblemished pale face, her well-cut hair.

She snatched a lipstick from her pocket and hastily smeared the plum colour across her beautifully-shaped mouth. She tossed her head and ran her fingers through her natural waves to give her coiffure a wilder look. She strolled, self-consciously casual, into the garish refreshment room.

Shouts of greeting came from the group around the jukebox. Four youngsters kitted out in black leather, their hair in various shades of pink and green and all wearing eye make up. It was only the lack of stature, a slightly different stance, one hip pushed out to the side, which distinguished one of the group as a female.

"Hi, Sal, what kept you?"

The toughest looking boy reached out and pulled her into the circle. As one of the others fed coins, pushed buttons, music blared out and the pair began to dance.

Half an hour later, as the others revved up their bikes more loudly than necessary, Steve locked up the café, of which he was the manager. Then he leaned on his big, black machine and pulled Sarah close to him.

"C'mon Sal, don't hold out on me ..."

"You promised you'd bring a helmet for me."

"Aw, c'mon - who's to see at this time of night - no cops about. And it aint far to Andy's place - c'mon - we can't miss out on a rave ..."

Paula tossed and turned under her duvet: she could not hold on to the comfort of her dream. Half-awake now, she tried counting guests, going over menus, checking off all the details of tomorrow's reception. But suddenly a nightmare took hold - a taxi racing along twisted narrow streets, roaring and sputtering at the corners, turning suddenly into a churchyard, hurtling towards an empty grave, a yawning black hole, the vehicle toppling over and spewing out a body to lie at the bottom, a twisted, bleeding form - a very still form. Too still! Like the shape in her daughter's bed! Paula sat up in her warm bed in the pleasant little bedroom. She could still hear the roar of a distant engine, real, not part of her dream though possibly the inspiration of it. She threw back the covers, dragged on a peignoir and stepped across the tiny landing.

She switched on the light - and Sarah rolled over and sat up blinking, clutching the covers close to her chin.
"What's wrong, Mummy?"
Had her little girl been crying, wondered Paula - or had she recently been scrubbing her face?

"I'm not sure." Paula hesitated. "Probably nothing but - I thought I heard something."

She moved over to the dress and gently shook out its full, flowing skirt. Her hands lingered on the soft, silky material.

"It's all right, Mummy," whispered Sarah. "Nothing can go wrong now."

Paula sat down on the edge of the bed.

"Sarah ..." she began.

Sarah took her hand.

"Mummy ..."

If only they did not find it so difficult to communicate.

"Were you in love with Daddy?" asked Sarah, making a huge effort to overstep the barriers between them.

Paula rose and went over to the window. She owed her daughter a truthful answer to this on the eve of her wedding, She stared into the darkness.

"I tried to love him, Sarah." She pressed her forehead against the coolness of the window pane. "But he was such a - disappointment - and then, leaving us so badly off when he died ..."

CHAPTER TWO

Paula Hanley was exasperated

"So, that's really all there is!" she said to the solicitor.

She slapped down on his desk the Last Will and Testament of her late husband.

"He led me a miserable life, scraping and saving, always ploughing everything into the business - the rewards were supposed to come later. And he didn't even make proper provision for us in case of his death."

Mr Steele looked shocked. Tom Hanley had not amounted to much, it was true, but he was hardly cold in his grave. Still, widows did react in some strange ways - he looked fondly at the photograph on his desk of his rather plain little wife. Surely my Milly will mourn me more then this, he thought.

He looked up and could not help but compare the face of his wife with the strikingly-beautiful Mrs Hanley. I wonder what she ever saw in poor old Tom in the first place, he thought. He remembered the wedding and the slight air of mystery surrounding the bride's background. Tom's family had made all the arrangements so everyone had assumed that Paula had no family and had been brought up a fair distance from this East Midlands town.

"Oh well," said Paula now, standing up and gathering up bag and gloves, "I'll have to make the best of it. First I must sell the house - one of Tom's foolish notions, buying a place he couldn't hope to keep up."

Mr Steele opened the door for her. She frowned at him as though he were partly to blame as she added, "But one thing is certain - Sarah won't suffer - I'll scrub floors before she has to go without."

As Harry Steele closed the door behind her he could not help but smile. The thought of elegant Paula Hanley on hands and knees wielding a scrubbing brush was just too funny.

But he was wrong in his estimation of her. Behind her careful grooming and fastidious façade, Paula Hanley was an extremely practical person. She had had to be because Tom Hanley had sailed very close to the wind in most of his ventures. There had been times when Paula had resorted to some painstaking tricks to disguise the fact that they were living in the shadow of a huge overdraft. Appearances had to be kept up for their daughter Sarah's sake. Thus

Paula would continue to give dinner parties for the parents of Sarah's peers and the female guests who never did a hand's turn in their kitchens or behind a vacuum cleaner would never have believed that their elegant hostess had polished her own silver and cooked most of their delicious meal single handed. Their husbands were always impressed by the way this beautiful woman made their every comfort seem her first priority and, to a man, expressed sincere envy of Tom Hanley. They all admired the elegant little jewel of a town house, bought impulsively by Tom on hearing that his uncle had bequeathed him his small business. This had long since been dismantled to pay off Tom's debts, incurred through a mixture of bungling incompetence and sheer laziness. Without exactly telling a lie, Paula had allowed people to believe that they had sold the factory because Tom was in poor health and needed to take things easy. The house remained in good repair thanks to a relative of Paula 's - her second cousin Jack. His wife, Mary, helped Paula with the housework and enjoyed acting the part of maid at Paula's dinners. Neither Jack nor Mary would have dreamed of "letting on" that they were family. They were a happy-go-lucky pair, content with their comparative poverty, Jack drifting from one job to another, daughter

Jane, like her father, disappearing now and then to take temporary jobs but always returning to help out, like her parents when needed at "our Paula 's posh place."

For Paula was not, as her neighbours imagined, from distant climes - she had crossed the tracks, as it were, into the high society of this little town, from a very poor part of it - a slum, if truth were to be told. She had clawed her way out of a background she detested - helped initially by her exceptional good looks and natural grace and intelligence - and even Tom was only dimly aware of the effort involved and the methods employed. As to her kith and kin, no one closer than Jack had survived to middle age and it was due in part to the bitterness of watching both parents and several uncles and aunts waste away under the evil influence of industrial disease that Paula found the determination to carve a better place for herself and her progeny. To Mary and Jack she was a fairy tale princess. With no wish to "climb" themselves they remained as Fate had decreed, enjoying a vicarious taste of glamour as their cousin triumphed. Paula herself, like many people who have elevated themselves, tended to be condescending and proud with members of the working class with whom she came in contact. But with Mary and Jack there was no such attitude. The discretion - secrecy even - was all on their side though when she realised that they genuinely wanted to keep in the background of her life, to make no public claim on her, she accepted gratefully their humble devotion.

Young Jane was polishing the mirror in the lobby when Paula returned from the solicitor's.

"Bad news?" she asked, seeing Paula's grim face.

"I'm afraid so, Jane," said Paula, pulling off her gloves. "All this will have to go."

She glanced regretfully round the tastefully-decorated hall.

"Ooooh, where will you go?" asked Jane. "Not too far, I hope."

"It'll have to be the country," said Paula. picking up the newspaper. "I should be able to manage a small cottage."

"Cor - Mum 'n Dad'll be upset!" exclaimed Jane. "Me too, o'course. We all love comin' over here."

She too looked round the room, at the carefully chosen furniture, lovingly polished.

1"Jane!" said Paula, lightly touching the girl's arm. "I've hardly paid you anything all these years - but now I can't afford even that."
"What about your Sarah?"

Paula's face tightened.

"Sarah's life must change as little as possible," she said.

"You mean she's to go to one o' them posh Finishing schools still?" asked the wide-eyed Jane.

"Perhaps not exactly a Finishing School," said Paula. "But whatever else has to go -Sarah must get her chance."

Jane turned back to her dusting. She, like her parents, worshipped Paula - she never thought of her as Aunty Paula or Cousin Paula. It was as if she had learned as an infant a noun synonymous with grace and perfection - the word - Paula.

But this adoration did not extend to Sarah. Jane was not jealous of the other girl, so near her own age and leading such a privileged life. She just wished that Sarah would show more appreciation - of her advantages and of having such a wonderful mother. She discussed it with her own parents when she got back that evening.

"Look, luv," said sensible Mary Jepson. "Sarah dunt know she lives in t'lap o' luxury - 'cos she's never known nowt else."

The plump, jolly little woman slapped her husband on the back. "Ee - it'd oppen 'er eyes to come ovver 'ere for a bit, 'ouldn't it, our Jack?"

Their small house was fairly clean but anything but tidy - yet Mary liked to keep Paula's house in perfect order.

Jane sighed. It rankled with her a little, not that she had to live in such dreary surroundings, nor that Sarah was kept away from the squalor of this end of the town - but that her mother should see all this as perfectly reasonable. Jack guffawed,

"Aye, lass," he said, taking out his pipe, a sure sign that he was about to tell a joke. "But it'd never do ... "

His voice and face were deadpan but Mary waited breathlessly for the punch line.

"Too much o' a shock might mek 'er ladyship wet 'er knickers!"

Mary shrieked with laughter and thumped her husband on the back again in appreciation of his humour. Then her face changed.

"Ee bur I don't know 'ow Paula'll manage - ee, that rotten Tom 'anley - I allus felt like kicking 'im up the backside."

"Ey, now, lass, tha musna speak ill o' dead!" admonished her husband.

Jane grunted. "Well - we didn't see very much of Mademoiselle Sarah Hanley before - I don't suppose I shall ever see her again."

****

It was only a few months later before Jane Jepson next saw Sarah Hanley. It was at a dance in a very rough part of the seaside town where Jane had taken a job at a hôtel for the season. There was a commotion on one side of the room and Jane went over to see what all the racket was about. A girl was dancing on a table, hair streaming loose over face and shoulders. Her decidedly sensuous movements were directed at a young punk, sitting astride a chair. It was only when she tossed back her mane of blonde hair to reveal her somewhat bleary-eyed face that Jane recognised Sarah.

CHAPTER THREE

Sarah paid off the taxi and took her first good look at Fernleigh Manor Academy.

Academy. What a pretentious and old-fashioned name. Those were also the best words to describe the building. Sarah shuddered. She may have failed most of her "O" levels but she had done brilliantly in the History of Architecture course and she recognised this as pure fake. Touches of Greek here and there, a mock Georgian window or two and a massive front door overloaded with badly-matched brass fittings added to, rather than distracted from, the total ugliness of the façade.

Sarah reluctantly pressed the electric bell and tried to feel grateful to her mother for sending her here. The fees were more than Mrs Hanley could afford even after drastically re-budgeting. But instead of giving up Paula had simply set about thinking out more economies. Sarah had finally realised what sacrifices her mother was preparing to make in her own personal comfort and had tried, but miserably failed, to convince her that she would be more than willing to go somewhere cheaper.

The door opened and revealed a pretty, vivacious girl a little older than Sarah.

"Another lamb to the slaughter?" she cried. She leaned towards Sarah and whispered. "Actually I was just making my escape - can't stand the place a moment longer ...''

"Oh!" Sarah was startled.

"No, no!" interposed the girl quickly. "I'm just kidding. *Chacun à son gout*- you might love the place - and I can give you a few hints on how to lessen the pain. Come on in. I'm Carol Blake. Here, give me your case. I'm not really running away."

Nevertheless she seemed to stare longingly down the drive before closing the door.

"This way to the Lion's Den!" she chuckled.

She led the way into a Mock Tudor hall, complete with Regency wallpaper and knocked on the first door.

A voice boomed out, "Come!"

Carol opened the door and ushered Sarah inside.

Behind a huge oak desk sat Hilda Schreiber, proprietor and tutor-in-chief of Fernleigh Manor Academy. She was a big woman in every sense of the word. Dressed in a very mannish suit, her massive shoulders needed no extra padding. Her huge head with its uncompromising Eton crop was fronted by a wide, flat face, unsmiling, aggressive.

"Miss Hanley?" she inquired.

"Yes," said Sarah. "I'm Sarah Hanley."

"Sit down, Miss Hanley. I remember your mother when she came down to - ah - ARRANGE matters. You couldn't accompany her, I recall - CHICKENPOX, wasn't it?"

Without waiting for an answer she reached into a drawer, still talking.

"Yes, yes, I remember your mother - so CHARMING."

She picked out a brown folder and leafed through its contents.

"Didn't do well in the "O" levels, I see."

She stared across the desk and this time it seemed she expected an answer, if not an explanation.

"No," said Sarah.

"Your mother seemed to think it was because you were still upset - ah - about your father's death."

"Perhaps," whispered Sarah, rather taken aback by this somewhat brutal reference to her recent bereavement.

But in fact she knew that as an excuse it had no validity whatsoever. Daddy had been such a remote figure in her life, she being away at boarding school most of the time albeit a school not too far away from home and where most of the well-to-do girls of the town spent their teens. During her holidays he often seemed to be away on what were vaguely described as business trips though nothing much ever seemed to come out of them. And when he was there he was always so tense and nervous, Mother had always tried to keep her out of his way with murmurings about business worries. He never seemed relaxed or light-hearted and often seemed to have difficulty focussing his attention on what was being said to him. The fact that she would never see him again had only just begun to sink in.

"Well now," went on this dragon of a woman, and for the first time she looked Sarah full in the face. Sarah was petite but there was a sinewy strength about her slight form. Her features were small and dainty but there was a hint of determination around her mouth. It was the face of a character as yet unformed. Miss Schreiber could hardly refrain from licking her lips and rubbing her hands together with satisfaction for here was a personality in the raw, so to speak. Unfinished, in fact. And Miss Schreiber's speciality was Finishing. A business college, devoted to training in secretarial skills was how her establishment was designated, but she and most of the parents of her students were well aware that it served its purpose as a cheaper way of grooming their girls for life - preferably a life of luxury. Her large face relaxed a little and she smiled. Sarah knew then what Carol had meant when she referred to the Lion. The smile may have started off inside her mind as a warm sign of proffered friendship but it finished up on the outside as a threatening, hungry snarl.

"We don't put too much emphasis on EXAMS here," she said.

Whoops, thought Sarah. So much for the Academy part of the name
....

"But we do aim to prepare our GIRLS for WOMANHOOD"
continued Miss Schreiber. The repulsive grin had disappeared and
Sarah decided that she preferred the fierce yet distant expression that
replaced it. She wished the woman would not talk in capital letters: it
tended to make Sarah shut off her ears to the main flow and just hear
the heavily-stressed words.

DEPORTMENT - FIRST IMPRESSIONS - SOCIALLY
ACCEPTABLE - HIGH STANDARDS

Whatever does it all mean? thought Sarah.

DECENT SOCIETY - GOOD TASTE - HIGH CLASS

Then suddenly something about the choice of phrases touched on
distant echoes in the girl's mind and Sarah was hearing her mother's
voice - " ... decent people - beauty and taste - unostentatious comfort
- freedom from financial worry."

On the rare occasions when Sarah was at home alone with Paula, the
girl had longed for heart-to-heart talks as described by her fellow
boarders after the holidays. But Paula was always filling Sarah's
hours with arrangements. She was to swim at the Blake's pool in the

afternoons, play tennis on the Redford's new court in the evenings, go riding in the mornings with the Mumford girls. From time to time when there was a breather from all this carefully-plotted activity Sarah would try to force a moment of confidences on her mother. She recalled one occasion when, catching Paula in a distracted mood, as she whipped up a special dessert in the kitchen, she embarked on a school anecdote.

"Julie Grainger was gated last term for being in the Library after hours."

"Sarah - you don't really want to be in here - you'll get your dress splashed with egg," tried Paula, then, as her daughter did not budge - "Grainger? Her father is a banker. isn't he?"

"Yes - she was marking all the rude pages in 'The Complete Shakespeare' ..."

"Well, don't drop her, dear. If she's a good friend - but don't break the rules just because she does - first impressions are so important, you don't want her introducing you to anyone as a fellow prankster."

Another time Sarah said. "Sheila Crowther was rude to Sister Martha."

"Crowther? Oh yes - they have the biscuit factory. She seemed a pleasant girl - she recited at the Concert, I recall - such nice deportment too - - perhaps Sister Martha misunderstood - still, it's good she has high standards."

"Lesley Greenaway made us split our sides doing an imitation of Father Thomas."

"Greenaway - oh yes, the scholarship girl - it's not very kind to mock people , you know. I don't think you should get involved with a girl like that - she's obviously not used yet to decent society."

1Sarah struggled to get down to basics. One day she remarked, "Nancy Martin's sister's been sent away to Cornwall. Nancy thinks its because she's having a baby."

"I'm quite sure it's nothing of the sort. You girls shouldn't be thinking of such things. Why don't you practise your French on each other - you'll need it if we send you to a high-class school in Switzerland."

"Oh, Mother - we can't work all the time. We've got to have a gossip and a giggle."

"Gossip! What a vulgar word. And nothing looks less attractive than a giggling schoolgirl. You have such a sweet smile, Sarah - don't distort it with silly giggling. And that reminds me - we must do something about your hair tomorrow - it's too long now and I've noticed you allowing a strand to stay in your mouth - that's not socially acceptable, you know."

Paula was always ready to advise her daughter on matters of style and taste but if Sarah showed her a passage in a book that had struck her imagination or tried to ask about anything approaching the biological - the Interesting Side of life as her friends called it - Paula would always plead tiredness and retire to her room to rest.

"Shall I play you my new record?" asked Sarah.

"I can do without noise just now," shuddered Paula, busy arranging roses in a silver vase. "But that reminds me - the Turners are making up a party to go to the Festival Hall - I accepted on your behalf."

"Oh, thanks," muttered Sarah. "What's being played?"

"I've no idea," replied her mother, "but the Turners are very friendly with the Higgs-Gracie family - their boys are sure to be in the party."

Boys were often included in Paula's arrangements - but only boys from the very best families and usually in large groups. And if, while watching television Sarah expressed admiration of some young pop star's looks, Paula would at once switch off the set. Finally she sold it - just another one of her ways of trying to shield Sarah from the vulgarity and ugly realities of LIFE. Even during the most recent holidays, when the move to the cottage was being negotiated, Paula insisted that Sarah should be spared any tiresome participation. She never dreamed that Sarah, jarred by the death of one parent might crave her mother's company at this time. She had been sent to stay with a succession of school friends, first to avoid the unpleasantness of the funeral and later the messy mechanics of the move itself. Sarah might have welcomed the fun of such an operation: her mother insisted that it was more important to cement relationships with her more influential friends especially now that there was no question of her accompanying them to the Swiss Finishing School on which Paula had set her heart for years. It was to be the much cheaper Fernleigh Manor for Sarah but first a short stay at the cottage was necessitated after all by the wretched chickenpox Sarah had caught from the young brother of one of these wealthy girls.

Only the best brand of chickenpox, of course, Sarah had remarked grimly to her reddened complexion reflected in the mirror of the little room her mother had so carefully furnished for her. She had not been very ill but had felt herself a burden on Paula who had worked like a slave to make the tiny house attractive and spotless and yet, miraculously, kept herself as well-groomed and meticulously neat as ever. She disciplined herself in front of Sarah ensuring that while the girl would lack no comforts she would have not even a glimpse into the extra labours that went into providing them. She made lots of new clothes for Sarah, none of which looked at all lumpy or home-made for she stayed up late finishing them off exquisitely. During Sarah's final few days at home she sat by the fire in the evenings watching her mother bending over some hand-sewing - dainty lace edging on lingerie - much nicer than most of her well-to-do friends had possessed.

"You're going to such a lot of trouble, Mother," ventured Sarah. I hardly like to say this ..."

Paula looked up anxiously.

"Don't you feel well, dear? You could stay a bit longer ..."

"I feel fine, Mother - but I wanted you to know - I don't have to go to Fernleigh. I could stay here and - and help out."

Paula put aside the pale blue petticoat.

"Sarah, believe me, you'll help me most by going off to Fernleigh and - and learning about Taste - Standards - Deportment ..... and typewriting, of course."

Sarah tore her mind back to the present. Yes, indeed, Miss Schreiber's briefing had reminded her of her mother. Could they then live by the same creed? Impossible to believe when you compared their appearances. Two women could not have been more different. That hideous smile - Sarah was shocked as she suddenly realised that she could not in fact remember ever having seen her mother smile. Was she so terribly unhappy? Sarah wondered if it were her fault. Was she a disappointment. But no, she did remember often catching her mother looking at her tenderly, indulgently. The corners of that shapely mouth just never turned up. Briefly Sarah had a picture of Mary waving a mop about in the big, bright kitchen and screaming with laughter at one of her own jokes. Paula had shaken her head reprovingly, indicating Sarah's presence and Mary had switched off at once, always anxious to please her idol.

"YOUNG MEN ...," Miss Schreiber was saying. Sarah pricked up her ears - something interesting at last. "End of term dance - ONLY THE BEST FAMILIES ..."

Sarah was sickened. So - that's what she's on about, she thought. How to make a good catch. That's what Finishing is all about after all. Finding the right husband.

She moved her chair restlessly. Miss Schreiber came to an abrupt halt. She stood up.

"ANY QUESTIONS?" she demanded and glared down on Sarah from her immense height.

She must be over six feet, quailed the slight girl.

"No thank you," she said meekly.

"Then I'll get one of the - ah - girls to show you your room," she said, and pressed a bell on the wall.

It was not long before Carol appeared, suggesting to Sarah that she must have been hanging about nearby.

"Ah - are you Duty Prefect, Miss Blake?" asked the Principal and her tone was decidedly cool.

Carol nodded and turning her head away from Miss Schreiber, daringly winked at Sarah.

"I can - ah - trust Miss Hanley to you, then," said the Principal coldly. "Here is your Schedule, Miss Hanley."

She handed Sarah a leaf out of the brown folder and sat down again at her desk. The girls went out together, jostling each other in the doorway and smiling about it. Once in the hall, with the door firmly closed behind them, Carol nudged Sarah in the ribs and clapped one hand to her mouth while pointing to the lion's den with the other. Sarah, too, could hardly stifle a shout of laughter. Once out of her damningly overpowering presence, Miss Schreiber became - unbelievable! Carol shook her head in warning and, taking Sarah's hand, led her upstairs.

They met no-one on the way through the many long, bleak corridors which led to Sarah's room but neither felt free to give rein to their feelings till they were safely inside behind the closed door. then both let out their shouts of hysteria.

"Whoo - oo - oo," gasped Carol, collapsing on the bed. "Well - here it is, my dear." Then, after her laughter was exhausted she sat up and said, " That was your dee- reck-treece and here is your sharm bra coo shay!"

Sarah could not imagine how she would be able to endure Miss Schreiber, she was extremely doubtful about being able to put up with Fernleigh Academy, But of one thing she was sure - she was going to like Carol Blake and hoped she would help to make life here bearable.

CHAPTER FOUR

At about the same time Carol was showing Sarah her room at the college. Paula was showing George Hanley the spare room tucked behind the kitchen in the cottage.

"It's very small, I'm afraid," she said. "But I'd rather not disturb Sarah's things - you do understand, I'm sure - I like to keep her room ready for her - for the holidays - and if she's ill .... "

"Sarah ill!" scoffed George. "Last time I saw her - School Sports Day, wasn't it - she was bursting with health and energy."

Paula shrugged her shoulders.

"With young people you never can tell. She contracted chicken pox quite recently."

"Poor kid! But anyway, don't worry about it," said George, ignoring Paula's coolness which was manifested by her extra-careful choice of words.

Contracted chicken pox, eh? Why couldn't the woman say caught chicken pox like everyone else?

"I'll be fine here," he went on, then decided to try to break through the ice. "If there's nowhere else for me to sleep ... " he added, taking Paula by the shoulders and gently turning her to face him.

She shook off his hand.

"Now, George, please don't start that again. It's not - decent - you're my brother-in-law."

George spread out his arms in mock disbelief.

"You mean - you'd fancy me if we weren't related!" he exclaimed.

Paula pushed past him.

"I must get the dinner started," she said.

George leaned into the tiny bedroom, flung his overnight bag on to the camp bed and followed her across the kitchen.

"Let me help!" he offered. "I'm a dab hand with an omelette."

"Omelette! Hum! I've never seen you cooking!" said Paula.

"There's lots of things you've never seen me doing," chortled George. "Just give me the chance ... "

As Paula frowned he continued. " ... a chance with your egg whisk, I mean."

He hung his head in pretended shame.

My God, he was thinking, Paula is hard work, she really is - not a glimmer of a smile ...

He almost wished he had not succumbed to his spur of the moment decision to call on Tom's widow. But he was so seldom in this part of the World, it would have been churlish. And besides, there were memories.

As it was obvious he had no intention of leaving her in peace to prepare the meal, Paula waved him to the breakfast nook.

"Sit down, George. Would you like a coffee while I dress the salad?"

"Er - got anything better to offer?" asked George, squeezing his bulk into the corner banquette, " ... in the way of a drink, that is," he added hastily.

"Oh, George, you haven't changed," said Paula.

"How's that?" asked George, who thought he had detected a shade warmer tone in her voice.

"Your teasing - and your drinking," explained Paula.

"You don't have to worry about me and the booze," he said. "I've not got the same weakness as Tom."

"Please ..." her eyes were pleading.

"Sorry, love, I didn't mean to upset you. Don't you want me to talk about him?"

"I'd rather forget all about your brother."

Now she was decidedly bitter.

"Bad as that, eh, at the end?"

Paula opened a cupboard and took out whisky and a glass.

"At the end - in the beginning - right through the middle!" she said.

"Crikey!" George poured himself a generous measure.

"Water?" said Paula.

"Please. About up to here. Well, well, so life's not been too good to you, Paula. And I've been no help, dashing about in France and Germany and Lord knows where."

"It wasn't up to you to do anything," said Paula sharply. "Your uncle was quite unfair to you - handing over the business to Tom and nothing for you."

George shrugged.

"The old boy just didn't like me," he said. "That's how it goes. I probably fell over his gouty leg when I was a lad."

"Or Tom did and made out it was you," suggested Paula. "And what a waste! I'm sure you would have made a go of it."

"Paula! Praise for old George! I can't believe it."

He half rose but Paula quelled him with a look.

"George, if you don't stop this I shall ask you to leave."

"Just what you said twenty years ago at that house warming party - do you remember?"

"Yes ... " Paula thoughtfully stirred her coffee. "I often wondered - did you go off abroad because of ..."

"No!" growled George. "Well - perhaps partly. I really admired you, Paula, it wasn't just a flirtation. No - I suppose I was sulking a bit about the business. I hung about a while to see if Tom would offer a partnership - then that other chance came up - so off I went."

"And we haven't seen a lot of you since," remarked Paula, who had just realised that here she was, entertaining a man who though in the strict eyes of the law was closely related to her was in fact almost a stranger. And she had no wish to entertain male strangers - she had quite a different, well-ordered, independent style of life planned out.

George, encouraged by the dreamy look in her eyes, leaned across the table and put his hand on her arm.

"No - it's been few and far between," he murmured. "But might I say - each time I see you - you are lovelier than ever."

Paula pulled her arm away and went over to the draining board to fetch the salad. Slapping down the bowl she said once more, in her coldest tone - "George!"

That night George lay on the narrow bed thinking about Paula upstairs. A terrible thirst crept over him and he quenched it from his leather flask. But a deeper thirst prevailed for the woman upstairs who reminded him of his youth. She had questioned him, over dinner, a meal far removed from the candlelight supper he had had in mind - she provided no wine and he thought it prudent to keep his flask hidden. She had asked why he had never settled, never married. Did she really not know, cool, silky Paula, how she had spoiled other women for him? He groped for the flask. Very soon it was empty.

He lurched his way to the foot of the stairs and listened. Not a sound, yet he was as aware of Paula's physical presence as if she were standing naked on the landing looking down at him. He made his way very slowly, cautiously, up the narrow stairway and stood outside her door. She was breathing deeply - he could hear her through the wood - she must be fast asleep.

I wonder ... mused George. Could I get away with it?

He pushed the door gently. It resisted. He gingerly turned the knob and, like a safe-breaker, listened intently for the click of the latch. Then he eased open the door and stepped inside the dark room. The heavy curtains shut out the moonlight but after a few moments George managed to distinguish the form of the bed and his senses quickened as his eyes traced the outline of Paula's body under the covers.

Two steps took him to the edge of the bed. He lifted the bedclothes and slid underneath. For a man who had recently consumed a flask of good Scotch, George had managed thus far with admirable subtlety. But his intentions were anything but admirable. He was counting on the recency of Tom's death to work for him in his dishonourable intentions. He stole closer to the warm, perfumed, female body, pressed himself up against her and let one hand creep over and begin stroking her arm.

Paula was in the middle of a vaguely-disturbing dream of a formless variety - she stirred and moaned softly. George held his breath. She restlessly tossed her body over so that she was now facing him. George caressed her face and touched her hair with his lips. Paula snuggled into his embrace.

My God, it's working, thought George. She thinks I'm Tom - and that side of the marriage must have been OK, it seems.

Paula's cuddle became a convulsive thrusting. She flung her arms round George and pulled his head down on to her breast.

"Please ..." she cried.

Then George made his fatal mistake. He spoke.

He intended to pour out his pent-up feelings for her in words ...

"Oh, Paula, my darling girl, my love, how I've worshipped you - now I'll show you what real loving is - wh-what the ..."

The voice had jarred its way through Paula's subconscious desires - she was suddenly aware of the horrific invasion of her sanctum. Opening her eyes wide, she shoved George away so violently that he fell in an undignified heap on the floor.

"Get out - you - you unspeakable creature," she shouted, leaping to her feet and glowering at him from the far side of the bed.

George crept on all fours to the door, mumbling apologies.

"Oh, God, Paula, I'm sorry - don't know what came over me - drunk too much ... "

"If it weren't the middle of the night, I'd throw you out of the house and your bags after you," said Paula, whose voice was now low and frighteningly-controlled. "I need hardly add that I expect you to leave first thing in the morning and never, never, I repeat, never - come here again."

George was now half way down the stairs and he heard Paula's door shut firmly.

"But Paula," he cried, hanging on to the stair-rail, looking back up the stairs. "Aren't I to see my niece? There's so much I can do for Sarah ..."

From behind her closed door Paula spoke icily. "You will never see Sarah again."

It was just a few months later when George saw Sarah. It was at a bar in a very prosperous part of the town where she had lived with her parents. George had been staring broodily into his glass for an hour when his attention was aroused by a commotion in the next room. There was so seldom any kind of disturbance in this plush hotel that George wandered, glass in hand, to the doorway. Two ruffians, one clad completely in black leather, were facing each other, broken bottles at the ready. The manager was remonstrating with a girl who seemed to be at the centre of the argument. She clutched at the lapels of the dinner jacket of the rather plump little man and tossed back her head while she screamed with laughter. The two boys suddenly lost interest in each other and decided to enjoy the spectacle of the older man's loss of dignity. The girl swung round and round in an exaggerated mockery of a waltz and it was then that her uncle recognised Sarah.

CHAPTER FIVE

Just as Sarah had hoped, she and Carol got on like the proverbial burning house. Unfortunately Carol was no favourite of Miss Schreiber's and Sarah had a fleeting sense of guilt that her mother might not approve of her pairing up with someone already established in a reputation for nonconformity.

Her fears were soon quelled when she discovered that her new friend came from a very wealthy and well-respected family. Paula could have no quarrel with that. Carol was not at one of the expensive foreign finishing schools for two reasons. She had been expelled from two of her boarding schools for breaking the rules so her people had to settle for Fernleigh where little notice was taken of previous performance. Also, she had her own motives, as yet undisclosed to Sarah, for wanting to be in this part of the country.

Sarah soon settled into the routine of the Academy - it was, as the Principal had boasted, an establishment devoted more to suiting the girls for their inevitable *niche* in society than to the nurturing of their minds. In fact Sarah, perversely perhaps, was more than a little frustrated at the meagre attention given to matters academic. The library was thin in good literature, no musical appreciation was encouraged, no outings to concerts or ballet and Miss Schreiber herself, theoretically in charge of the Arts, was clearly more interested in her own pursuits - golf and fishing. Walls and shelves in her study and any odd little nook or cranny in the corridors were festooned with her trophies - cups and statuary as cumbersome and lacking in grace as she was herself. She seemed quickly to lose interest in her newest pupil but Sarah did notice that she paid a lot of attention to a particular group of small, timid girls. "Natch!" said Carol when Sarah remarked on this. "You know why, don't you?"

"No," said Sarah, who up till now had come into contact with adult women of two types only - those who resembled her own mother or those who wore the nun's habit. Sarah, at seventeen, was very unworldly, unaware of the wide variety of character and type in the human race.

Carol winked.

"I'll fill you in later," she said. "I can see you need some real practical education, my girl."

Reluctantly Sarah had to leave it there because she was due for her English Literature lecture with Miss O'Grady - and here she had found an inspiring combination of a subject and a tutor she liked. Books had clicked with her in spite of rather than because of the guidance she had previously received. She felt confident that she was going to get on well with this one teacher at least who seemed eager to guide her.

"Together we can share the rich experience of our literary heritage," said Siobhaan O'Grady in her introductory talk. "We will start, of course, with Shakespeare - but there are many other worlds to discover between these covers. She turned to the bookshelves. Then her sweet-featured face twisted into a wry grimace for they were studying in the Library and Miss O'Grady shared Sarah's first impressions of its limitations.

After just a few tutorials, Miss O'Grady took to addressing her more profound remarks and opinions directly to Sarah. On her part Sarah made a point of arriving early and leaving after the rest of the group whenever she could manage it. The teacher gladly made it clear that she was more than willing to make freely available to this responsive student her own personal collection of books. Carol expressed disapproval.

"Watch it, that's all - don't get sucked into any traps," she warned, "She's Authority too, you know, however much she appeals to you at the moment - in my opinion she could be more dangerous than the lion."

"Dangerous!" echoed Sarah incredulously. "Miss O'Grady! Why, she wouldn't hurt a fly. She's often on the point of tears when we come to a sad bit in a novel."

"Oh, my poor little Sarah," said Carol, half-playfully but with an underlying gravity. "I must give your Special Syllabus some serious thought."

"Hmm?" muttered Sarah, who, though very fond of Carol and her happy go lucky attitude was often puzzled by her friend's enigmatic remarks.

"The Syllabus concerning your Preparation for the Big, Wide World, my dear," said Carol, deepening her voice in a marvellous imitation of Miss Schreiber's gruff tones.

" ... To hell with DEPORTMENT and LE CATCHING OF LE ELIGIBLE HOMME, I'm going to arm you against LIFE'S DANGERS, don't you know ..."

"Oh, Carol, you are a scream!" laughed Sarah, as usual completely disarmed and deflected from pressing her to further explanations by the light-hearted entertainment she provided in the build-up.

1"Sorry I can't stay and amuse you further," said Carol suddenly brisk. "I have important business to attend to - you will sign in for me, won't you?"
Sarah sighed as her friend flung out of the room. She was becoming rather concerned about these escapades. The girls were allowed two late nights each month and to accommodate this privilege there was a rota of duty monitors who sat up in the lobby after lights-out in order to unbolt the side door and let in the late comers. It was relatively simple to swap duties if a friend expected to overstay the 11.30 curfew, then sign her name and slip a latch on a back window.

This was the third time Carol had jauntily persuaded Sarah to be an accessory to her flaunting of the rules.

Sarah followed Carol to her room and stood in the open doorway watching her friend frantically brushing her short, dark curls. She tried to reason with her.

"Carol - all rules are made for a reason," she began. "Even here at Fernleigh."

"Wubbith and Nonthenth!" giggled Carol who had had Geography that afternoon with poor Miss Beatrice Parkson whose unfortunate lisp she frequently copied. "It'th jutht to thtop uth having a good time."

"No, Carol - they are rethponthible - I mean responsible - oh, Carol you'll have me talking like that in class one day - they're responsible for our safety. They put their trust in us twice a month but they must make sure we are back at a reasonable hour."

"Why?" asked Carol in wide-eyed innocence.

"Well - if we are not back it could mean that something bad had happened."

"Dahling gel!" said Carol, who seldom spoke without using someone else's voice and had now switched to that of the Sports Mistress, a very horse and hounds person. "What in the world ken heppen to us arfter 11.30 that kennot heppen befoh?"

"No, no!" Sarah laboured on, trying to make Carol see another point of view. "I mean - if we've agreed to be back by a certain time they can assume that after that time we are not back because we've had an accident."

"Oh - an accident ... " breezed Carol. A certain glint in her eye made Sarah think along other lines.

"Look, Carol, I know it's none of my business - but why do you have to be out till all hours?"

"Right!" snapped Carol. "None of your business."

This was so unlike her that Sarah blushed deeply and her eyes filled with tears. Volatile as ever, Carol rushed over and put an arm round her.

"Shucks, kid, I'm sorry," she said." Just - can't talk about the dark side of my life - not just yet anyway, eh luv? Forgive me?"

"Yes of course," said Sarah. "I just get so confused - you see, Mother allows me out till midnight sometimes during the hols but quite honestly I start yawning about half past ten and wish I was safely tucked up in my cosy bed."

"Ah yes, luv - but who are you with on these boring occasions?"

"Oh, usually a party of people - sons and daughters of people Mummy visits."

"EGGS - actly!" said Carol. "Now, when you're with someone really interesting who opens your eyes to the wonders of the world - time just means nothing and at eleven thirty you've just begun to ... no, I must leave it there - anyway you've made me hours late already. I must fly. Bye ..."

At eleven thirty Sarah dutifully forged Carol's signature. The other monitor had gratefully accepted Sarah's offer to finish the waiting up alone and crept off to bed. Just as Sarah closed the book and pushed back her chair, she felt someone's breath warm on her neck. Thinking that it was Gillian returning to remind her that the forbidden hour had arrived, Sarah spoke without turning.

"It's OK - I'm just packing it in myself."

Sarah gasped as the person behind leaned over and reopened the book. She was even more astonished when she realised that it was not the book that was being perused - flicking it open seemed to have been just an excuse for bringing her face close to Sarah's. Sarah's heart thumped. It was the face of Siobhaan O'Grady.

"Sarah!" breathed the young woman, in mock reproach. "Up so late? You'll be far too tired to enjoy our little session tomorrow - you haven't forgotten, surely?"

Her voice seemed to be pitched lower than usual - yes, it was definitely - husky. Was she sickening for a cold, wondered Sarah - or just tired after a day's teaching and an evening's marking. There were dark rings under her eyes, certainly. But the eyes themselves were sparkling - and held a look Sarah could not give a name to - but it frightened her. Involuntarily she drew back and Miss O'Grady straightened and made room for her favourite pupil to lift back the chair and stand up. Thankfully Sarah realised that if it had been her intention to check the Late List, she now seemed to have forgotten. "Come," said Miss O'Grady, lightly touching the girl's arm. "I'll see you back to your room."

Sarah felt sick with fear. Firstly, she wondered if she could hope to get away with creeping back downstairs after making sure Miss O'Grady had returned to her own quarters. Secondly she felt an undefined menace from this person with whom she had imagined herself up till now in an excellent pupil-teacher rapport. Small and neat, angelically pure of face, yet something nasty seemed to emanate from her in the dimness of the great, draughty hall. Sarah's instincts warned her to be on her guard but against what she had no clear idea.

"I- I'll just check the bolt on the side door," she said. "Don't trouble yourself to wait for me, Miss O'Grady - you look tired."

The teacher pushed back a strand of hair uncharacteristically straying from her tidy chignon.

"No!" she protested harshly. Her grip tightened on Sarah's arm. "The door is quite secure. I can see from here."

Sarah gathered up the small pile of books with which she had whiled away her duty hour. Miss O'Grady reached for the topmost. Sarah noticed that though her hands were small and dainty her fingers were long and slender. They curled over the book like so many snakes.

"Ah, you're reading my D.H. Lawrence," she said, as though in laying claim to the book she was asserting some sort of right over the borrower.

They walked slowly up the stairs and along the dimly-lit corridors, Sarah suppressing a scream yet somehow aware that if she were to lose control and let it out, drawing attention to the situation, she would be hard-pressed to explain herself to anyone who responded.

Then suddenly a shaft of light was flung out into the shadowy gloom and the massive form of Miss Schreiber appeared in the doorway of her bedroom.

"Ah!" she said, and Sarah tried to store up the forceful comment contained in the single syllable to reproduce for Carol later.

There was so much about tonight's events that she could not sort out in her own mind, she was determined to pin down Carol as soon as possible and beg her to explain all her previous hints and innuendoes because somehow Sarah believed that was the only way she would be able to understand the weird behaviour of these two strange women. Yet now - Sarah became unsure again - were they so odd after all - or had Carol's exaggerations for the sake of getting laughs planted the idea in Sarah's mind. Had she read too much into Miss O'Grady's attitude - it could be also because she was overwrought with the fear of giving Carol away that she had misjudged her teacher. Yet the two colleagues were surely glaring at each other too fiercely for two ordinary women? They switched their gaze to Sarah.

"Off to bed now," said the Lion. "I presume you've just finished a Late Duty?"

"Yes, Miss Schreiber," said Sarah and lost no time hurrying on up the next flight of stairs.

She heard the Principal say in an unnaturally loud voice - for Sarah's benefit obviously - "And you look as though you need your bed, Miss O'Grady. I'll say goodnight."

There was the sound of the door being closed and Sarah was grateful to have reached her own sanctum. She shot the bolt behind her and leaned on the door, listening. She was relieved to hear the slippered shuffle of Miss O'Grady as she made her way to the West Wing.

About two hours later she became aware of a tapping on the door. After fighting off sleep when she had finally got into bed, fully intending to pluck up courage enough to sneak down to the back window when the coast was clear, Sarah had finally lost the battle and succumbed to a mixture of thinking and dreaming. Her conscious musing was an attempt to work out exactly why she had been afraid of Miss O'Grady. She had tried to visualise the woman honestly - a dowdy little college lecturer in a demure, high-necked housecoat, plain carpet slippers on her unremarkable feet, her hair in a simplified version of its daytime bun but thinner, more meagre, probably devoid of its doughnut-shaped "rat" foundation. But into this rational assessment kept creeping the vision of those long, white fingers fastening on the book but seemingly aching to close round Sarah's hand. And those eyes piercing Sarah's face as she bent over her, seemingly striving to get across some message too intense for words. Not surprisingly her consequent dreams had been full of writhing snakes and swirling, misty, formless horrors. But at last she had to acknowledge the reality of the knocking on the door especially when it was accompanied by a voice.

"Sarah! It's me, Carol - open up."

Sarah sprang out of bed and let her in. She was dishevelled, eyes red-rimmed and swollen.

"Oh no!" moaned Sarah. "You didn't get caught ..."

"Yes, my little friend," said Carol but by her look she bore no malice.

"I'm truly sorry," sobbed Sarah. "I honestly meant to go down and open the window."

"The window ... " said Carol in a strange faraway voice. "Oh no, luv. I came in by the front door. Didn't you - don't tell me you haven't heard all the commotion. There's ears at every keyhole and faces at every crack along the corridor."

"Wh-wh-what ... " stammered Sarah and began to rub wildly at her eyes as though trying to ensure she was not still dreaming. Carol pushed her further back into the room.

"I've only got a few moments," she said and again her tone was detached, remote. "Try to get a grip on yourself - I've come to say goodbye."

Sarah sat down on the bed. The room seemed to be closing in on her. Carol sat down next to her.

"I've only one regret, my poor silly little Sarah," she said, "I shan't be able to take on your HIGHER EDUCATION after all."

"Wh-wh-where are you going?" asked Sarah, still trying to stifle her sobs. "

"Oh, I'm not sure - Paris, Rome, Japan - where doesn't matter, my love."

"Are you - running away?" asked Sarah.

"Not really - more a case of being taken."

"But - were you caught or not?"

"Ah yes - but I wanted to be caught. I rang that old bell as bold as brass."

For a moment the old familiar mischief was back.

"You should have seen the Lion's face! What a picture! And your precious Miss O'Grady was just as funny."

"Both of them?" questioned Sarah and her heart sank as she faced the inevitable prospect of recriminations from the two women in the morning.

"Oh yes, indeedy!" triumphed Carol.

She cocked her head to one side and then darted over to the door, opened it a smidgeon and stood listening. Sarah thought she could discern a distant shouting - Miss Schreiber's angry boom - and a man's voice. Suddenly Carol darted over to her and kissed her.

"Take care, my lovely Sarah," she said - and was gone.

Sarah felt unable to move for a long time. Tears streamed down her face and she was only half aware of the sound of doors slamming and a car driving off. Slowly she got up and closed and bolted her door. Then she lay down and pressed her face into the pillow and cried herself to sleep.

The Academy was buzzing at breakfast. Oddly, Sarah noticed that the whispering stopped in each group she approached. Miss O'Grady did not appear at High Table where there was as much huddled speculation going on as in the rest of the room. Finally Miss

Schreiber entered, though usually she was not present at this meal, taking her breakfast much earlier. She strode straight to the centre of the room and forks and spoons ceased clattering.

"Young LADIES!" she said. "I would like to make an ANNOUNCEMENT before GOSSIP and RUMOUR get out of hand and take a HOLD of your IMAGINATION. Miss Blake has been expelled from Fernleigh Manor Academy. You will not see her again and, take my word for it you will be BETTER OFF without the possibility of the BAD INFLUENCE which might have been brought to bear on you. It would be better to forget you had ever come into contact with such a PERSON."

Sarah stared at her plate while the Principal was speaking but she raised her eyes to watch the daunting figure in her plus eights (one of Carol's jokes describing the tweedy suit of enormous proportions the woman wore every day) stamping out of the room. Then, as she became aware of everyone's eyes on herself, she surmised that Miss Schreiber must have directed her final remarks in her direction.

On her way out Sarah nearly collided with Gillian Marriott.

"What a carry on, eh?" said Gill.

"You mean about Carol?" said Sarah.

"Mmm. You signed her in last night, didn't you?"

Sarah hesitated but Gill had always shown herself to be a good sort. She nodded.

"Well, I know you did," smiled Gill, "'cos I rubbed it out just now - thought it would be for the best - in the circumstances."

"Thanks," mumbled Sarah. Gill leaned close.

"I've heard she ran off - with a married man," she said.

Sarah muttered something about being late for lessons and made her way quickly to the privacy of her own room.

CHAPTER SIX

Paula put the finishing touches to the white vase of yellow daisies on Sarah's dressing table. She stepped back to admire their simple beauty. A gentle breeze stirred the dainty dralon curtains - the room had a fresh, innocent appeal.

She glanced out of the window as she heard a car turn into the lane from the main road. Yes, it was a taxi: it must be Sarah, back for the half-term holiday. Paula glided down the narrow staircase and opened the front door to welcome her daughter. Sarah hurried eagerly up the path. How good it felt to run towards her mother - a normal, feminine woman. And how cosy the small, trim cottage appeared after the forbidding, unsympathetic architecture of Fernleigh Manor.

She tried to hug her mother but Paula held her at arm's length.

"You look well, darling," she decided. "Did you have enough money to pay off the taxi?"

"Of course, Mother - I don't know why he's still there ..."

Sarah looked back to where the cabdriver was indeed taking an unconscionably long time to turn the vehicle in the lane. She realised that he was staring at Paula with unconcealed admiration.

"I do believe Fred March fancies you, Mummy," said Sarah.

"Please, darling, don't be vulgar. And how do you know his name, may I ask?"

"Sorry, Mother," whispered Sarah, instantly deflated. "He told me - and now I come to think of it, he was fishing for information about us - about you, I should say - Mother, you definitely have an admirer there."

"Come inside."

Paula's arms took on the aspect of enveloping wings as she once again tried to protect her daughter from reality. But Mother Hen or not, she could not resist sneaking a glance back over the hedge. Fred March, a personable fellow in his mid thirties who ran his business from the Council Estate near the station, was making a great to-do of adjusting his wing mirror. Realising his ruse had been penetrated, he first began to blush then plucked up enough courage to brazen matters out. He stared in open admiration at Paula - and winked. Paula caught her breath, then returned his stare with an ice-cold scrutiny that made him drive off with a screech of tyres - but he continued to smile to himself.

When Sarah had been reinstalled in her room and had washed away the travel dust she was, as always, anxious to chat with her mother. She cornered Paula in the tiny sun-room built on to the back of the house. Paula kept her sewing machine here and, as Sarah poked her head round the door, her mother hastily bundled some material into a basket.

"Oh, don't stop!" cried Sarah, squeezing herself past a small table and sinking into a cushioned garden chair which totally filled the remaining space. "I'll sit here while you sew and I can tell you all about Fernleigh."

Paula took a small scrap of lace from a drawer. She began tacking it on to the edge of a dainty garment.

"What's that?" asked Sarah. "It looks like a nightie. Is it for me?"

"Of course!" said Paula defensively. "This is the last of the old lace your father's aunt gave me before she died."

She held up the beautiful old French trimming to the light.

"They had such lovely things," she sighed. "That branch of the family could have done so much for you, Sarah. Now there's no-one we can turn to, we must make our own way."

"What about Uncle George?" asked Sarah, unaware of the outcome of his recent visit. "Did he turn up? How was he? He used to take us on such jolly picnics, I remember."

"Nonsense, Sarah. He took us on one outing to Cambridge, that's all."

"B-but - he hired a punt for us," said Sarah, taken aback by her mother's sharpness. "And we had asparagus rolls and strawberry tarts - and champagne, I seem to remember."

"Probably!" sniffed Paula. "Now - what were you going to tell me about Fernleigh?"

Suddenly the past few weeks seemed different to Sarah. She tried to tell it as it had happened but it came out in quite another light.

"There was this super girl, Carol," she began. "She was a lot of fun but she got expelled - for - staying out late ... Then there are these two peculiar tutors - the Principal, Miss Schreiber and the English lecturer, Miss O'Grady - they're both so weird ..."

"Really, Sarah," interrupted Paula, "you do pick up the most awful slang. And remember I've met Miss Schreiber - how can you call her - weird - her family were German aristocrats. And you yourself wrote during your first few days about Miss O'Grady and made her sound a very nice, cultured sort of person. And as for this Carol girl - I'm shocked that you should have befriended someone like that. I shall have to inquire into this business of her expulsion - you weren't out late with her, were you?"

Miserably Sarah shook her head in denial and felt that she was betraying her friend. Paula, after all these corrections, did not like to see her daughter so completely subdued into melancholy. She decided to drop the subject for the moment.

"Let's talk about something cheerful," she suggested. "Somewhere around here I've got the brochure about the skiing holiday ..."

She began pulling out drawers.

"I've arranged for you to travel with the Willards - you know, those two sisters who live in that perfect little Georgian house opposite the rectory."

Glumly Sarah answered. "Yes, they're about ninety each, aren't they? I should be safe enough with them."

"Safe! I should hope so."

Paula stopped searching for the leaflet and looked at her daughter.

"Sarah! Surely a mother should try to ensure that her daughter is - safe."

"Yes, Mother, only - I'd much rather you came with me - not two old spinsters I hardly know at all."

"Nonsense, Sarah - they're younger than I am. Not forty yet, certainly. I know they are a bit reserved and old-fashioned but they were so eager to help when I mentioned your holiday in Switzerland - they have a time-share chalet in a very nice resort."

"... and what do I need to go to skiing resort for, anyway?" asked Sarah sulkily.

The usually tightly-controlled Paula seemed flustered and managed to tip over her sewing hamper. Out spilled the material she had been working on when Sarah arrived - a rather gaudy cretonne. "Whatever's this hideous stuff for?" asked Sarah, fingering it gingerly. Paula began once more to stow it away.

"Just some curtains," she said. "Ah - here's the brochure - it had got into the hamper. Let's take it into the living room. This place gets chilly once the sun moves round."

Sarah followed but her thoughts remained with the material hidden away in the basket. Her instincts told her it was the sort of stuff the Willards would smother their windows with - was her mother taking in sewing to provide the means to send Sarah abroad? She was certain that her suspicions were correct but she was equally sure that her mother would hate to have to admit it. She could not quite bring herself to force her mother's confidence on the issue but the idea of the expensive holiday was suddenly abhorrent to her.

The following day the Willard twins called at the cottage. Sarah spotted them in the front garden as she was gazing moodily out of the window, having been yet again banished from the kitchen and her mother's company. They were bending over to inspect the bronze chrysanthemums. She ran downstairs.

"I think it's the Willard sisters outside," she said.

She watched her mother closely for signs of a guilty reaction which might give more proof of her demeaning relationship with them.

"That is, unless you know more than one pair of twin females past their first youth."

"Hush, Sarah," said Paula. "They are not hard of hearing, however ancient they may appear to you. We don't want to hurt their feelings."

Sarah half expected her to behave like a serf, flustered at a visit from the Lord of the Manor to her humble abode. But exactly the opposite happened. Paula took off her dainty apron without haste and glided gracefully to the door to receive her guests. It was she who displayed self-assurance, even a touch of *hauteur* while the two maiden ladies coloured up and gabbled away in acute embarrassment at having been caught out snooping around the flower beds. Paula took pity on her visitors.

"I'll cut you some of my chrysanthemums to take home," she offered kindly. "They're too crowded anyway."

"Oh, thank you, thank you," said Miss Fanny.

"You are too kind, my dear Mrs Hanley," echoed her sister

"Do come inside and talk to Sarah," said Paula. "I'll make some tea."

"Sarah dear, you do look well." gushed Miss Isobel. "Fernleigh must suit you."

"We went there, you know," said Miss Fanny, settling herself fussily into an armchair.

Sarah was thinking to herself that these must be the last two women in the world still wearing lacy gloves to go out on calls. Then she realised what Fanny had said and impulsively responded.

"Oh - it's been going that long, has it?"

Fanny put a pale thin hand up to her mouth to hide her shocked little exclamation but Isobel seemed to have more spirit. She laughed - a girlish chuckle.

"Oh yes - for a hundred years at least - but actually we went there about twenty years ago. It was quite *avant-garde* for gels to go to Business College in those days, you know."

She was shaking her head at her sister as though to explain that allowances must be made for the generation gap. Fanny instantly got the message, as often happens with twins.

"Goodness, yes, it does sound a long time ago, doesn't it?" she said. "And yet - it seems only yesterday we were packing our trunks to come home for the hols."

Sarah slid down on to the rug and rested her elbows on a *pouffé*. Suddenly, even in jeans and T-shirt, she felt an affinity with these two in their georgette frocks and lace-trimmed hats. They too had experienced Fernleigh. Perhaps she could communicate her vague misgivings about the place to them.

"Did you know Miss Schreiber?" she asked.

Then she bit her lip in exasperation at her own *gaucherie*.

"Oh no!" she cried. "There I go - putting my foot in it again - she couldn't have been Principal then ...."

Seeing another chance of lessening her worries by sharing them slipping away she added dejectedly "Nor Miss O'Grady - you wouldn't have known her either."

"Oh yes," said Miss Fanny. "We knew Siobhaan O'Grady."

"Hm! And Hilda Schreiber!" added Miss Isobel grimly.

Sarah sat up, startled.

"Siobhaan came just before we left," explained Fanny. "As a student. We heard she went back there to teach after University, didn't we, Isobel?"

"Yes, dear. And we heard about Hilda Schreiber taking over from Sylvia Cranley."

Paula came in with the tea tray. She served everyone in her usual neat, efficient way.

Then - "You were talking about Fernleigh, I suppose," she said. "Isn't it funny, Sarah - I didn't know Miss Fanny and Miss Isobel when we chose Fernleigh but of course it isn't too far from here so I suppose it's not that much of a coincidence."

Sarah felt piqued at the way Paula kept addressing the sisters as Miss Fanny and Miss Isobel but then she remembered Fred March, in the taxi - the twins had just emerged from the churchyard - "There go Miss Fanny and Miss Isobel," he had said. "Been visiting their relations, I see."

But his voice had held a note of affection. Sarah had the feeling that the whole village was fond of the eccentric pair. She had heard that they had run the Sunday school for years and they were very generous to all the local charities. On the one hand they seemed immersed in their own quiet life in this sleepy corner of the country yet they were quite *blasé* about foreign travel. Fernleigh must have done something for them, thought Sarah, but it certainly could not claim to have made them into Women's Libbers. They seem to have been more sheltered even than she had. She shuddered at the prospect of becoming like them, firmly frozen into the pattern of a bygone age, content with each other's company.

"Sarah seems to be doing well at English," said Paula, handing round scones. "Miss O'Grady has taken quite an interest in her, it seems."

Was it her imagination or did Miss Fanny pause, halfway through biting into her cucumber sandwich - and look anxiously at her sister, wondered Sarah.

Isobel spoke drily.

"Yes - Siobhaan was always reading - liked to hear her own voice - would insist on reading poetry aloud to the rest of us - I like to enjoy it privately myself."

Sarah began to listen more intently to the conversation for it suddenly seemed that the sisters were saying something between the lines, as it were. Paula seemed totally unaware of these undercurrents.

"You were saying Miss Schreiber was there with you as well," she said innocently.

"She came to teach Sports and Accounting," said Fanny with a shudder that clearly expressed her memories of those items of the curriculum.

"And Siobhaan was her shadow," sniffed Isobel. "Extra coaching in tennis, she got - and of course she was Captain of all the college teams,"

I can't imagine her wielding a hockey stick, thought Sarah, let alone tackling the Lion.

"Yes," mused Isobel. "And Schreiber made poor Sylvia's life a misery. Turned the whole curriculum upside-down. No cultural pursuits, no exams - and precious little real training in shorthand and typing. Then her father - a Count, it was rumoured - died and left her a tidy sum and she persuaded Sylvia Cranley to sell her the school and move out."

Paula's interest in the personnel of Fernleigh Academy had dwindled. Abruptly she changed the subject.

"Do you always go to Switzerland in the Winter?" she asked.

"Yes," replied Fanny. "We've had a share in the chalet since we were teenagers, you know. We've always loved travelling ..."

"And Sarah is very welcome to stay at the chalet," said Isobel. "If she is at all unhappy at her hôtel - sometimes these days, the people at the resort are - you know - not very - quiet."

"Oh, surely," began Paula, who was pinning such hopes on this holiday for her daughter. To her it was of far more importance than the syllabus at Fernleigh - an extra "finishing touch" she was determined to provide.

"Yes, yes - of course," said Isobel. "I keep forgetting that young people don't like to be quiet. Well, we musty be going. The Vicar is coming to supper."

"And to lunch tomorrow," said Miss Fanny with a sweet smile - and followed it up with a coy look at her sister.

Good grief! thought Sarah. So there is Romance in their lives!

Crikey! - Fancy beginning at their age.

She could not make them out - she was on the verge of liking them but - they seemed worlds apart from herself.

Paula was seeing them to the gate. They were arranging something, looking back towards Sarah. Isobel called out.

"Sarah dear - come to lunch tomorrow - your mother says it's all right - she's kindly offered to send flowers for the table."

Fanny hung back and putting her gloved hand up to her mouth she added in a stage whisper -

"Yes, do come and help me chaperone my sister."

I just don't get it, decided Sarah. Surely those two are not as - simple - as they seem.

But as they turned at the corner of the lane to wave, Isobel winked - as broadly as Fred March had winked at Paula. Sarah decided that, understand them or not - she liked the odd pair.

CHAPTER SEVEN

Sarah woke late and basked in the midmorning country sounds for five luxurious minutes. Cows mooed lazily in the distance, somewhere nearer a horse clop-clopped along the lane and right outside her window a blackbird chirped his hymn of praise for this fine Autumn day.

This peaceful background medley was suddenly shattered by the harsh scream of a pneumatic dill. Then a lorry tipped out its clattering contents. Hammering, banging, raucous male voices followed.

Sarah was just about to go over to the window to investigate this horrific cacophony when Paula bustled in with a breakfast tray. She set it down and hurried across to close the window and draw the curtains.

"That will shut out some of the noise," she said, shuddering. She handed a cup of coffee to her daughter and made for the door.

"Oh, Mummy, stay and talk while I have breakfast," pleaded Sarah.

Paula frowned.

"I have a million jobs waiting downstairs," she objected.

"Oh please - Mother," said Sarah. "At least stay long enough to tell me about that horrible row."

Paula sat down on the dressing-table stool.

"I can hardly bear to think about it," she said despondently.

"Someone has bought the old petrol station on the main road - no-one ever used to call there - it was so inconspicuous with that lovely old ivy-covered wall hiding it from the road ..."

"Goodness!" laughed Sarah, her mouth full of toast. "Wh'd wnt t'by splaysh li' 'at?"

"Sarah! Don't speak with your mouth full!" remonstrated her mother. "What have they been doing with you at Fernleigh?"

"Well, actually, Mother, I was going to talk to you about that ..."

She took another bite of toast and Paula returned to the subject that was her pet hate of the moment.

"The firm who've bought the place are re-styling it - the old wall was demolished immediately - it always reminded me of the enclosed garden at Oakley Hall - you know, we were invited once to a Garden Party - you remember the Burton girls at school - their place - I think there was a peach tree trained up it ..."

The sound of another load of stones being shot out penetrated the room despite Paula's precautions, and rudely interrupted her reminiscing. She shuddered as she harped back to the desecration of this spot she had so carefully chosen for its remote tranquillity - where she had hoped to lie low and lick her wounds, unobserved.

"There's to be a great forecourt for lorry drivers to park - some sort of cafe with a jukebox - to attract youngsters of a certain type, I suppose."

"Oh, Mother," teased Sarah, "you are a snob!"

Paula blushed. Sarah could not remember ever seeing her do that before.

She could not guess at the connotations the word held for Paula. How many times had her contemporaries said it to her and of her during her long struggle to rise above their unacceptably low standards. All except Mary and Jack who, whilst acknowledging their incapability, and indeed their total lack of ambition, to achieve any other life style than their comfortable, slovenly background, nevertheless sympathised with their beautiful cousin in her desperate striving after a better existence.

"I wish you would trust me, Sarah," she said now. "I know which people are worth something in this world and which are totally useless. If that is being a snob - well, yes. I am one and that's all there is to it."

"Oh, Mother, I'm sorry," said Sarah, her love for her mother gushing up in her though she could not begin to understand the anguish behind her words. "I didn't mean to criticise. I know how ignorant I am."

"What do you mean - ignorant?" asked Paula, indignation chasing away her emphatic but appealing wistfulness. "How can you be ignorant after all I've taught you - and paid for others to teach you?"

"No, no, Mother!" protested Sarah. "Not that kind of ignorant - though you must admit I made a right mess of my "O" levels. No, what I meant was - I know nothing about Life - the World - Carol was always telling me I was - innocent. Yes - innocent's a better word."

"I should think so, indeed," said Paula drily. "A girl your age should be concentrating on self-improvement, developing her character - there's no need whatever for you to try to be ... "

"Experienced?" offered Sarah.

"Your Carol seems to have had more than her share of that," said Paula. "A good thing she has gone out into the World she seemed to know all about - and not stayed on to be a bad influence."

Sarah flung herself the length of the bed to be nearer her mother.

"There are other - influences - inside Fernleigh," she confided. "Not all the bad people are outside!"

Paula looked startled and Sarah was overjoyed to feel that at last she was on the brink of finding a way to communicate her unformed fears to her mother. But the telephone chose to ring, as is often the case, at this very inconvenient moment which seemed to be leading to the intimacy Sarah craved.

Paula frowned, tried to ignore the ringing, leaned towards her daughter as if ready to pursue the subject she had only briefly recognised as a possibly real problem. But she had to give in to the strident command from below.

"I must answer it," she apologised and hurried out.

"Damn!" said Sarah, and taking her mother's place at the dressing table, began vigorously brushing her hair.

In a few minutes Paula was calling up the stairs. "Sarah, that was Isobel Willard on the phone. They'd like you to go over earlier than we said - to meet some relative of the vicar's, I gather."

Oh no, thought Sarah. Not another old maid - probably his decrepit sister. Or worse - someone young they've picked out as a little pal for me - some lank-haired niece with a lisp ....

Paula was waiting in the narrow hallway with the door already open when Sarah, dressed deliberately casually, in trousers and sweatshirt, came running downstairs. Paula did not bat an eyelid at this obvious contrast with the style of the Willards.

"I've just the scarf to go with that sweater," she said. "You know - the Liberty silk. It's in this drawer, I'm sure. I'm so glad we bought those French-cut slacks," she added, as she pinned the scarf neatly into place with the brooch she had been wearing herself.

She handed Sarah a neatly-wrapped brown-paper parcel.

"Is this too heavy for you?" she asked.

"What is it?" Sarah dared to ask. "The crown jewels? We could always ring for Fred March's taxi."

Paula took her seriously.

"I suppose we could ... " she began.

"Oh, Mother - it was a joke! Of course they are not too heavy."

She watched Paula's reaction to her use of the word "they" to see if she realised Sarah had guessed about the curtains. But Paula showed no signs of agitation.

"I've a basket of flowers ready too," she said. "Will you be able to manage both?"

Just then a car drew up outside and to the surprise of mother and daughter they saw the vicar alight and make his way up the path.

"Mrs Hanley - how nice," he muttered, holding out his hand. "And this must be Sarah. How d'you do. Er - Fan - er that is, Miss Willard

- asked us to pick up Sarah - you see my nephew arrived last night - he drove me to the Willard residence - ridiculous seeing that they live so close - I think he's bursting with pride in his new motor car - er - the two ladies remembered that Sarah was bringing - er ... "

He pointed at Sarah's burdens.

"Yes, yes!" Paula snatched the bulky bundle and thrust it into his arms.

"Yes, yes, that's right - er - no hurry - if you're not quite ready to come - Jeremy will wait," mumbled the shy fellow, backing off down the path.

"Goodbye to you for now, Mrs Hanley."

      Sarah was trying to get a look at the driver of the car without obviously craning her neck. Paula pulled her back into the house and made a pretence of putting the final touches to the scarf.

"Oh that Reverend Philpott," she whispered. "He really is impossible! I know he's not well off but really, his clothes are too shabby. And just look at that old banger his nephew is driving - new motor indeed! Shall we make some excuse, dear, so you don't need to go?"

But Jeremy had jumped out of his beloved vehicle to help his uncle and at the sight of his ash-blonde hair and tall, slim good looks, evident even at a distance, Sarah's heart had leaped within her and she felt a totally new sensation of giddy excitement. Paula, still fussing with her neck line, had not seen the young man.

"No, no, Mother - give me the flowers," said Sarah and, wrenching herself from Paula's busy fingers and holding the blooms close to her face to present as pretty a picture as possible, she ran down the path.

Jeremy was holding open the car door for her and as it was indeed a very old-fashioned model with a steep step up, he gently took her elbow. Sarah felt that she would faint at his touch. As they drove away the vicar introduced them with old-fashioned courtesy and then launched into a rambling account of the young man's life history but Sarah heard nothing. She was staring at the back of Jeremy's head and glorying in his thick wavy hair, his broad shoulders emphasised by a chunky Aran sweater, rather streaked with oil. As she gradually recovered from her new sensations she became aware that though the car was indeed old, it was anything but a "banger".

"Old cars are Jeremy's special interest," said the vicar. "He does them up, you know."

Oh crumbs, thought Sarah, now won't Mother be just thrilled that I've made the acquaintance of a garage mechanic - worse than Fred March even ...

They were driving past the petrol stage in its first throes of metamorphosis.

"What a mess!" said Jeremy, indicating the skeleton of the new building, the concrete mixers, the dust.

"Yes, indeed," said the vicar. "And what a pity that old wall had to go - it's completely changed the - er - character of this little corner."

"It'll probably bring more traffic too," said Jeremy, turning to glance at Sarah. "That will be rather annoying for your mother, won't it?"

He looked genuinely concerned.

He doesn't sound like a mechanic, thought Sarah, as thrilled by his well-modulated voice as she was by his good looks.

To her disappointment he delivered them to the Willards' gate and took his leave - he could not even stay for a drink after all and Sarah convinced herself unhappily that she was the cause of his sudden change of plans.

He just wasn't going to stand for being stuck in the company of an immature student, she thought. After all, he must be at least twenty two - probably put me down as a private school prig. He's probably rushing off to meet a sophisticate with bleached hair ....

She tried hard to despise him, to put him out of her thoughts. Fanny Willard was no help.

"What did you think of Jeremy?" she asked as she showed Sarah round the garden.

"I didn't really notice," lied Sarah, looking back at the gate where Isobel and the vicar were waving off the ancient but well-polished Bentley.

1"Let's go round the back," suggested Fanny, "and leave the two love birds together."
Sarah was shocked. But Fanny smiled and nodded and pulled her guest round the side of the house.

"Always making excuses to be alone, they are," she confided. "And whispering together in corners."

Sarah was just beginning to wonder if the woman was slightly deranged when she happened to glance at the windows of the house - and saw that the curtains were of exactly the same material with which Paula had been working - and that two of the lower windows were bare. Sarah was puzzled by her own emotions. Recently she had called her mother a snob yet now she felt truly affronted by the idea of her mother doing other people's sewing.

Fanny sat down on a seat under an old apple tree.

"Sit with me, Sarah," she said. "Tell me - what do you think of Jeremy?"

Sarah was disconcerted. Surely Fanny must be really off her rocker - repeating the same question so soon. It made it doubly difficult to answer: fortunately she was rescued from this dilemma by Isobel marching up to them.

"Fanny, dear," she said, " do go inside and help the house keeper with the last of those curtains."

"Where is Cy - where is your friend, the vicar?" asked Fanny nervously.

"Oh, go on with you, Fanny - Cyril's in the kitchen, making us some drinks. He'll bring them out directly."

Reluctantly Fanny went towards the house and Isobel took her place on the bench next to Sarah.

"Poor Fanny," she said - and then fell silent as though trying to remember something.

After a few minutes, Sarah spoke.

"You have a lovely house, Miss Willard."

"Call me Isobel, dear," said the older woman. " ... at least - when we are alone," she added.

Surely she can't be frightened of Fanny, thought Sarah. Not shy, timid, batty old Fanny.

"Ah yes!" said Isobel abruptly, recalling what she had wanted to say before. "About the curtains - you're upset, aren't you, Sarah?"

"Upset!" repeated Sarah, aghast at having her thoughts read.

"My dear, you are so lucky to be blessed with such a mother," said Isobel. "She has such skill with fabrics. In another life she might probably have been a dress designer - I 'll wager she made that - what is it they are called now - tee-shirt?"

"Yes, " said Sarah. "They are - and she did."

"But not the trousers - they are French, aren't they?"

Sarah looked amazed.

"You'd be even more surprised if I were to tell you I've been to the Paris Collections more than once, wouldn't you?" asked Isobel, laughing at Sarah's incredulous stare. "Oh yes, of course you would - seeing me dressed like this - and Fanny as well. Two figures from a Gainsborough painting, Cyril says."

Again she laughed heartily.

"Cyril! Ah, me - but we were talking of your mother - such good taste - and so alone - you are her whole life, you know, Sarah. So - if I were you I wouldn't harp on the business of the curtains - what she does she does for you - and take the advice of a silly old frump - she doesn't mind doing ... I say - just look at that!"

She interrupted herself to point towards the house, without actually turning to face it. Sarah stole a surreptitious look. At one of the empty windows the vicar was holding up a curtain while Fanny shook it into neat folds. His look was frankly adoring.

"B- but," stammered Sarah. "I thought ..."

"You thought it was me - after Cyril, didn't you? My dear, our families have been close since we were small children. And of course I'm fond of the soppy old dear - but he has eyes for no-one but Fanny - always has been that way."

"Then - why ..." mumbled Sarah.

Suddenly Isobel seemed to go off on a different tack.

"You will be careful at Fernleigh!" she said, looking very serious.

Sarah could think of nothing to say from such a non sequiteur.

"If anyone makes you unhappy - you won't put up with it, will you?"

Sarah began to get a glimmer of a connection between Fanny's

unfulfilled romance and her days at Fernleigh.

1"I wish I'd let Fanny run away when it came to it - then, perhaps,
she wouldn't be ...."
A loud crash muffled her last words. The vicar - the lovelorn Cyril -

on his way out to them with a tray, not as Sarah had expected, of

coffee - but with appetising-looking apéritifs - had stumbled and

dropped a glass.

"Oh, Cyril, don't cut yourself!" cried Fanny who was following with

a decanter.

Isobel turned to Sarah and - once again - winked.

CHAPTER EIGHT

When Sarah got home, she was bursting to discuss everything that

she had seen and heard at the Willards' but she could see at once that her mother was upset. Paula was sitting at her small oak bureau, agonising over a letter she was trying to write. A pile of crumpled sheets of pale grey note paper lay in the waste paper basket.

"What's wrong?" asked Sarah.

"Oh, Sarah, there you are - I was going to phone."

Paula sounded distraught.

"I've had bad news ... " she went on, standing up and heading for the kitchen.

"Sit down, Mother, you look so pale," said Sarah, barring her way.

"But - I'll make you some tea while I tell you," said Paula distractedly.

"No - let me make you something," begged Sarah.

Paula shrugged and twitched her mouth, dismissing the idea of Sarah being capable of such a task.

"Let me keep moving about," she said. " Come in the kitchen with me."

Sarah followed and did not even attempt to set out the cups in case it should irritate her mother.

"I've had a letter from Mary - in Chemster - Jack's had an accident - fell from some scaffolding on a building site - he doesn't seem to have broken any bones - but - he isn't getting better ..."

Paula sat down opposite her daughter and poured tea for them both. "Poor Mary isn't much of a letter writer but, reading between the lines, I think she's - frightened. She and Jack have always been so close."

Sarah's heart went out to her mother, sitting there looking so wistful. Was she comparing Mary and Jack with herself and Father - had she ever felt about him like Mary did about her husband - like I might feel about - someone - some day? wondered Sarah and her thoughts raced back to her first glimpse of Jeremy. She fought against the memory. It seemed so awful to dwell on that remembered thrill, that surge of warm, tingling joy - whilst her mother was relaying this bad news.

Suddenly Paula stood up.

"I must go to them," she said. "I'm sorry, Sarah, to have to spoil your holiday - but do you think you could manage for a day or two?"

"Why - yes -" said Sarah but she was nevertheless quite taken aback - one minute her mother was refusing to believe that she was capable of making a cup of tea - the next minute she was proposing to abandon her, leave her to her own devices. Sarah guiltily realised that she would indeed probably turn out to be quite hopeless at looking after herself.

"Couldn't I come with you?" she asked.

"Oh no!" said Paula instantly. "The house is too ... small," she finished lamely.

Sarah knew that what she really meant was - it was not good enough for her daughter. She could not fathom this contradiction - how could it be possible for the fastidious Paula to stay there - and yet be unfit for Sarah.

Paula was having second thoughts.

"Oh, dear, I just don't know what to do for the best - perhaps I'd better telephone the college and see if you can go back early - you did mention that some staff and pupils were staying over half-term, didn't you?"

"Ye - es," admitted Sarah. "But - really, mother - I'll be all right here, I'm sure."

"No -o," mused Paula, already moving to the phone. "I'll feel happier if you are in a safe place ... "

SAFE! thought Sarah, but could not bring herself to plead with her mother to be allowed to stay at home. However, as a last desperate effort to get the message over she went back into the kitchen and began noisily washing up. Two minutes later, Paula came back to find Sarah standing staring in amazement at the two separate pieces of a cup she had broken.

"Oh, never mind that, dear," said Paula, attributing the girl's trembling lips and tear-washed eyes to her concern over the breakage, seeing no deeper disquiet underneath.

"They weren't very good cups. I've just been talking to your Miss O'Grady. She will be very happy to have you back early."

Sarah suppressed a howl of anguish.

"Now - let me see ..." went on Paula.

For the first time that Sarah could remember she was pushing Sarah's needs to the back of other priorities.

"We must both do our packing - and I must phone Fred March to pick us up. No - first I must phone about train times ..."

Sarah felt it would be churlish now to add to her mother's worries by disputing her decision about Fernleigh - she slunk off to her room and began to throw clothes and books into her suitcase.

Paula came up half an hour later. She shook her head dolefully at the messy result on the bed. She tipped out the whole unorganised jumble and began carefully folding garments.

"There is something you can do, Sarah," she said, perhaps unaware that she was thus pointing up this further proof of Sarah's inadequacy.

"Can you write a little note to Miss Isobel telling her we 've got to leave in a hurry. I just don't know when I'll be able to get together with them to discuss your skiing holiday ..."

"Oh, but surely, Mother, now ..."

"What's that?" snapped Paula, coming out of her trance. "I do hope you were not about to say something foolish about giving up your trip."

Sarah would have liked to say exactly that - about the money being better used to help Mary and Jack - or even Paula herself. About the idea of a holiday abroad being much less exciting than the prospect of a chance meeting with Jeremy at the Willards' village home. About how sick and disgusted she was with Fernleigh.

But Paula had laid her plans carefully - and even in this unexpected crisis she would brook no discussion of alternative ideas for the well mapped out future she had laid before her daughter. Sarah knew now that it was no earthly good trying to put over her own point of view. She crept downstairs and wrote the note. As she was licking the flap of the envelope she heard a car outside. She lifted back the curtain and saw Fred March in his taxi.

Her mother came down, dressed as elegantly as ever in a well-brushed suit, carrying her beige leather suitcase.

"I've got to leave you here after all," she sighed. "My train goes at four - yours at six. Fred March will come for you. I'll take the keys so be sure to pull the door firmly to behind you, won't you?"

She pulled her daughter close for a few seconds and kissed her on the forehead.

"Sorry, Sarah - that I must go off in such a rush - I'll telephone the school tonight to make sure you've arrived safely. You've enough cash for taxis and tickets, haven't you - goodbye then ..."

1   Sarah waved her off from the doorway and observed Fred March, blushing like a teenager, worshipping respectfully this "lady" he was privileged to serve.

Back in her room, Sarah found her own case repacked and strapped, her coat and hat laid out neatly on the tidied bed. Idly she wandered across the landing to her mother's room and began picking up ornaments she had known ever since she could remember. Then, without realising the import of what she was doing, she began opening and shutting drawers. Suddenly she understood that this was a betrayal of trust, an invasion of privacy - but as she was about to close the drawer where Paula kept her scarves, she saw a piece of newsprint amongst them. Half-persuading herself that she believed it to have got there by mistake, Sarah took it out and unfolded it. It was a cutting concerning an accident to a young man who had been driving too fast on a mountain pass - there was a photograph of an Oxford undergraduate, smilingly unaware of his eventual untimely end. Sarah did not recognise the handsome, rather arrogant, face at all ...

Suddenly she knew that she was prying. She replaced the paper, closed the drawer, dashed downstairs, snatched the letter for Miss Isobel from the hall table and ran outside, slamming the door.

She had forgotten that it was on the latch. She just wanted to get outside, to try to disperse the growing feeling of a huge rift opening between her and her mother. For so long she had mildly resented Paula 's obsessive directing of her life and yet now that she was beginning to see her mother as a separate person with a life and a past of her own, apart from - even secret from - Sarah - she felt resentful, hurt, deserted.

She would walk as far as the main road and post the letter - there was a stamp on it which Paula must have automatically stuck on in her usual efficient, tidying-up-loose-ends way.

As she turned the corner of the lane, a motor cycle raced by, almost brushing against her - the shock made her stumble into the ditch. She picked herself up, recovered the letter, dusted herself down and then looked to see if the motorcyclist had swerved and lost his balance. No - he was all right. He had stopped - but only momentarily. Barely glancing back to see if she had survived, he satisfied himself that his machine was undamaged and, to Sarah's amazement, drove off again and turned in to the forecourt of the half-finished café.

Sarah was furious. She crammed her letter in to the post-box and marched across the road. She pushed past the bike, parked casually amongst the wheelbarrows and mixers. She stepped over the door frame, held in place by wooden props, and confronted the young man. He had taken off his helmet and was obviously waiting for her. Indeed, it seemed to Sarah he was thoroughly enjoying the whole situation - having a good laugh at her expense. And his hair was purple! It stuck straight up like a cockscomb. A punk!

"Hello, darlin'! Want summink?" he said insolently.

1"I jolly well do," said Sarah, trembling with rage. "I want an apology. You nearly killed me out there."
"Aht theah!" he mocked. "Eow! Hi sayh! Pahdon me."

Sarah's temper rose even higher. She went towards him threateningly, though hardly aware of what she meant to do. His arm shot out and a terrifically strong hand gripped her above the elbow. Then his other arm went round her. Next moment there was utter confusion - a shout, a crash - as the precariously-mounted door frame was knocked over and then the punk was lying on the dusty floor, his nose bloodied. Sarah turned to find Fred March, breathing heavily, dishevelled - and very angry.

"Come on, Miss Sarah," he said, taking her arm as gently as the other fellow had gripped it cruelly. "This is no place for you."
He led her out and they picked their way over bricks and spades and other clutter to where the taxi was standing, engine still running. He bundled her inside and drove off towards the cottage.

"Are you all right?" he asked as he turned into the lane. "Did he - do anything - hurt you?"

"No, no," said Sarah. "I'm fine, but how ...?"

"I was just driving by when I saw him - holding you," said Fred. "Here we are."

As they pulled up at the gate, Sarah realised that she was locked out - and her suitcase was inside.

"Anything else wrong?" asked Fred, gently considerate - Sarah deeply regretted ever having made fun of him.

"I'm locked out." She felt really foolish.

"Oh, cripes! And your train not due for an hour and a half," said Fred.

He jumped out and held the door open for her.

"Unless you'd rather me run you over to the Willards ..." he suggested.

Sarah explained about her luggage.

"Never fear - Fred is here!" he said laughing. "Let's look round and see if there's anything to be done."

For the first time in her life Sarah felt the warm sense of security that comes from being protected by a strong, capable male. Much as she wanted to love the memory of her father, Sarah had had to admit to herself that he had not matched up to the descriptions of other girls' fathers. Her mother had constantly struggled to shield her from the more unpleasant aspects of life but Sarah had nevertheless felt a gap, a lack, a difference - in her own life. Now here was Fred, who only days before had been a joke to her, almost someone to be despised - an unknown quantity from another species - yet here he was, making her feel safe and secure. Having so recently come into contact with yet another alien type of masculinity in the unfinished café she had a flash of understanding about her mother's reluctance to allow her daughter to be exposed to the World. But she felt that she could trust Fred implicitly and that he would solve any problem that arose.

In less than ten minutes Fred had located a slightly-open window, found a ladder, entered the house and smilingly opened the front door, inviting her jokingly to please step inside.

"Was there anything more Moddom required?" he said in a funny butler voice. With him the impersonation was no insolent mockery as had been the cruel punk's mimicry.

"You've been so kind," said Sarah - and though she had fully intended to join in his jovial mood - she burst into tears. Very gently, Fred took her hand and led her to an armchair.

"You sit there," he commanded. "You've had a shock. I'll make you some nice hot tea."

To Sarah's further amazement he reappeared in an incredibly short time with a tray as daintily-laid as one of her mother's offerings. And the tea he passed to her was delicious - if a little on the sweet side. She blinked at its sugary taste.

"Plenty of sugar they always say - after a shock."

He playfully wagged his finger at her.

"And I'm sure you've no need to worry about dieting."

He sat down opposite her.

"I'll just stay until you feel better," he went on. "The moment you want me to leave - just say the word."

Sarah thought he was looking anxiously out of the window towards his taxi.

"Oh - I'm keeping you from your work .." she protested.

"Nah!" he denied. "You're my next fare anyway - booked in for the six-ten train." He added hastily - "Not that I need hang around till then if you're feeling recovered. I don't want to be no trouble."

Looking at his kind, friendly face, Sarah wondered why people made such a fuss about class. So - Fred did speak ungrammatically - but what a kind heart he conveyed with his words - and she believed him truly honest and - honourable.

"Please, " she said. "Are you not going to have some tea?"

"Oh - all right, seeing as you've invited me!" he chuckled. "I'll fetch the other cup I put out just in case."

While he was out of the room, Sarah tried to define the difference between him and the punk who had treated her so dishonourably. Surely there were not that many stratas of society - Fred was a little older than the crude youth but he had probably been born into a similar background.

"Your mother really keeps things neat," said Fred, returning with an extra cup and a tin of biscuits. He blushed as Sarah looked suddenly wary.

" ...I won't beat about the bush," he began and Sarah felt panic-stricken.

Surely he was not going to declare his undying passion for her mother. Though she had joked about it with Paula, she was horrified at the thought of discussing it with Fred. Suddenly he was a stranger again, an unknown quantity. Then he broke the spell.

"I admit everything," he said. "I brought these biscuits in 'cos I didn't 'alf fancy one - but I'm sure it would be good for you to eat something."

Relieved that he was not after all going to launch into a confession of love, Sarah shook her head.

"No - but you go ahead," she offered. "Mother bakes them herself."

She could have bitten off her tongue. It was as if she were angling to invoke the very words she dreaded by extolling Paula's virtues. Indeed, Fred held his half-eaten biscuit in front of his face and lapsed into silent admiration of the dainty titbit.

"Cor!" he said at last.

Sarah uneasily tried to read his thoughts.

A beauty like her - and she can cook too, speculated Sarah, strangely irritated. She felt reckless. After all, the punk had tried to kiss her - he must have found her attractive. She crossed over and sat on the arm of Fred's chair.

"Anything Mother can do, I can do better," she declared, trying to imitate Carol's husky voice when she was doing her Marlene Deitrich impersonation.

Fred looked up at her, startled. This close, Sarah could see how immaculately-groomed he was. His hand, still reverently holding the half-biscuit, was very clean. The nails too were clean and well-cut. His hair shone with cleanliness and she could smell a fragrance new to her innocent and inexperienced senses - not just his after-shave lotion but what she supposed must be his - maleness. It was very pleasant.

"Why don't you kiss me?" she asked, but already she was beginning to be afraid, regretting her silly impulse.

Fred put down the biscuit and stood up. He laid his hand on Sarah's head. He looked own at the fresh, pretty girl - offering herself on a plate, as some of his coarser pals would have put it.

"Oh, Sarah," he sighed, and like an echo of Carol he added, "Someone 'll have to look after you - or you'll land in a whole lot of trouble."

Humiliated, Sarah sprang up and ran out of the room. She raced upstairs to her bedroom, slammed the door and stood leaning against it, listening. This has happened before, she thought, reliving the night when Carol was expelled. She half expected, hoped perhaps, that she would hear him coming up the stairs. What would she do then? Open the door wide? fling off all her clothes? Sarah was horrified to discover that one part of her longed for him to come and take her. Yet he had not stirred her heart as had Jeremy, to whom she had hardly spoken ten words. Maybe that's it, she mused unhappily. I so wanted to get to know Jeremy - I'm probably using poor Fred on the rebound. Or could it be that I am - jealous - of Mother ... She flung herself on the bed and wept, sure now that Fred would not follow.

Ten minutes later she crept downstairs, case in hand, to discover Fred finishing off the washing up. As she opened her mouth to speak he raised his hand in a forbidding gesture.

"Not a word!" he insisted. "Forget all about it. Folk react in some funny ways to shock. Let us be friends, eh?"

He held out his hand and smiled - such an engaging smile - Sarah knew as they 'shook on it' that he would be just that - her friend.

"Come on, now," he said briskly. "Let's see about getting you to the station. And - Sarah ..."

She looked at him, trusting him utterly.

"If you have any more trouble - and your mother's not around to help - here's my card - telephone me, won't you?"

"I've had my full share of trouble, I'm sure," said Sarah with forced lightness.

But - as the train drew out and she saw Fred's taxi, a symbol now for her of dependability, driving off in the opposite direction she knew she did not really believe that her troubles were over.

CHAPTER NINE

To Sarah's relief the first person she encountered at Fernleigh was Gill Porter who had had to stay over the half term as her parents lived abroad.

"Come on," she said eagerly to Sarah, "There's hardly anyone decent here - let's move your stuff down to my room - it's a double, you know."

"Fine," agreed Sarah.

She could not begin to express the relief this simple solution brought to her terror of being back at the Academy.

"Dinner's finished, of course," said Gill as they went upstairs.

"That's OK - I'm not hungry," said Sarah.

Gill made less tiresome the necessary chore of unmaking and reassembling bedding and transferring all the bits and pieces by a flow of excited chatter. After a while this struck Sarah as being uncharacteristic of the usually quiet, studious girl. She too was interested in literature and was keen to show her personal collection of books to Sarah. But her voice became more and more agitated as she talked about her favourites.

"I just love anything comical - Jerome K Jerome right through to A comedy of Errors - whoops - that should be the other way round I suppose ..."

Another surprise - for Sarah had supposed Gill's tastes to be more serious - philosophy, was it? No - she remembered - Gill had always been the one for poetry. Sarah picked up a volume of Keats and idly opened it. Miss O'Grady's name leaped out at her from the flyleaf. Gill snatched the book and shoved it untidily back on to the shelf.

11"I hate Keats!" she declared with a sudden change of mood.

"Oh, Gill, dear - how could you say such a thing?"

Sarah swung round at the sound of the familiar, softly-brogued voice. Siobhaan O'Grady stood in the doorway, a slight frown on her face. She looked so ordinary, so typically the plain schoolmarm. Sarah decided she must have exaggerated the stuff of which her nightmares had recently been fashioned.

"Oh, hello, Miss O'Grady," she said brightly. "I've just got back."

Miss O'Grady did not seem to hear. She moved closer to Gill who was, Sarah realised, trembling and pale.

"Now, Gill - how about a half-hour in the rose garden?" said Miss O'Grady.

She bent down and plucked out the Keats.

"It's a lovely moonlit evening. Let us go and rediscover this beautiful young poet together."

With scarcely a nod at Sarah she swept out of the room and Gill, head bowed, meekly followed.

Before Sarah had time to reflect on all this, Helen Meeks dashed into the room and closed the door behind her.

"Hello, Sarah, come to swell the ranks of the Undefeated?"

"Whatever do you mean?"

Sarah snapped open her suitcase. She had never cared for Helen - she, like Carol, often stayed out after curfew and Carol, who with hindsight Sarah realised had no right to criticise other girls, had warned Sarah that she was a "bad lot."

"Oh, come on - you know," said Helen airily. "Here - shall I help you unpack - you look dead beat."

Sarah wondered if she were just being nosy, wanting to poke around in her things. But no, it seemed a genuine offer and in no time at all Helen had efficiently stowed away everything in drawers and cupboards.

"Now you are safely installed and you can protect poor old Gill," she said. "I did tell her she was welcome to bunk up with us - but she's so timid - afraid of her own shadow and anything and every - except you apparently."

Sarah went to the window and leaned out, craning her neck to try to see into the rose garden but it was closely sheltered by tall, thick hedges. Helen came and looked over her shoulder.

"Hm, yeah!" she commented. "Talk about putting on the pressure. Poor old Gill came here, it seems, to escape from her father - he wanted her to be a missionary or a nun or something. And all she wants is a place in the real world amongst real people in an office

somewhere - and now o' Grady is pushing her towards some awful

exam to try to get into University. Still - I offered to introduce her to

some real people of my own but she doesn't trust me or my Douglas

any more than anyone else - so I gave up."

"Douglas?" queried Sarah.

Helen did not answer directly.

Instead she asked,"Did you meet any chaps in your short hols?"

Suddenly Sarah felt awkward, gawkish, immature.

"Two or three," she avowed, glibly.

"Really?"

Helen was looking at her with new respect.

"Any good? What type?"

"We - ell." said Sarah, terribly anxious not to spoil her new image,

"there was Jeremy - he's a business man."

"No go!" promised Helen. "Too stuffy!"

"And then there's Fred - " went on Sarah and encouraged by Helen's

look of interest, added boldly - "a taxi driver."

"What happened with him?" asked Helen, stretching out in Gill's

easy chair, filing her nails with Sarah's emery board.

"We were alone in the house for a few hours," said Sarah.

Helen sat up and took notice.

"Go on ..." she breathed.

Sarah felt a modicum of self-disgust. She should not betray Fred like this. Yet she so wanted to be in with Helen and her set - mostly to gain safety in numbers if she were to be ranged against the unnamed dangers of this place.

"There's this punk, too ... "

She waited for Helen's reaction.

"That sounds more like it!" she said. "Rough, is he?"

"Oh, yes," declared Sarah. "Very rough - he forced me to kiss him - he dresses in black leather."

"Go on with you!" laughed Helen. "You've made it up - you're fantasising. Now if it had been me telling it - it would have been true."

"No, really," said Sarah. "He drives a motorbike, a big one. We met in a - er - café - near my house."

"Well, sorry, Sarah - for not believing you - I must say I didn't think you had it in you - how about taking a late night pass with us sometime - I could introduce you to Doug's friend Reg."

"Are they boys from home?" asked Sarah.

Helen almost fell out of the chair, laughing.

"Oh, Sarah - you are a hoot!" she giggled. "My Aged P's would just die if they knew about Doug. They've had their hearts set on the "boy next door" for me since we were both three years old."

Sarah remembered that Helen's home address was Chadwick Grange - so exactly what did that make the boy next door, she wondered.

Helen was suddenly serious. "... and I shall probably marry Bertie," she said. "We were blooded together - he takes me to the Hunt Balls. Yes," she sighed. "I shall probably end up as Lady Haddon."

She stood up and went to admire her reflection in Gill's mirror.

"But in the meantime, there's Doug and - oh, Sarah - he's fantastic."

She ran her hands though her hair.

"I must fly - Marge is going to put blonde streaks in. I wonder if O'Grady will notice. Oh well - till she does ..."

She was gone and Sarah's head was spinning.

Oh why does everything happen at once, she asked herself. Why did I have to meet Jeremy - and Fred - and the other one - all in one day.

What do I want? Surely not a night out with Helen's Doug and Reg - no, no - surely not that.

Gill crept into the room, white of face, red of eye.

"Did she give you a telling-off?" asked Sarah.

Gill put a finger to her lips in warning. She closed the door cautiously.

1"Sarah," she said. "Will you help me? I'm going to run away."
"Gill," gasped Sarah. "Why?"

Gill shook her head and choked back her sobs.

"Please, Sarah - help me!" she begged.

"All right, Gill, if you're sure - but where will you go? Your people are in India, aren't they?"

"No - Africa - but I've an aunt - she's really sweet - I know she'll not turn me away."

"Where does she live?" asked Sarah.

"In the North. The Lake District. I've enough money for the fare. I just want you to cover for me till I get well away ... "

"I see," said Sarah doubtfully.

Complicity, deceit - these were new to her, foreign to her nature. She still felt badly enough about giving Helen a false impression of her own exploits - even though she had not strictly lied.

"What exactly do you want me to do?" she asked.

"I'm just taking a few things in a haversack," said Gill, beginning to grab bare necessities from her bureau. "Then I'll slip out the back way to the station on my cycle. Can you stuff some pillows down my bed in case - er - anyone - looks in?"

Gill stopped her packing for a moment and touched Sarah timidly on the arm.

"And if - anyone - does ask for me - can you please try to make them believe I'm asleep?"

Sarah insisted on escorting her downstairs to the infamous "laters" window where she stood for five minutes after the wistful little figure had disappeared into the night. She recalled Gill telling her once that she was afraid of the dark - so how much worse must be her fear of whatever she was running from here? Then Sarah remembered that the last train of the day left the little country station at nine in the evening. Gill would be stranded. It was vital that her disappearance should not be discovered till midmorning to ensure she got well away on the milk train.

Sarah was tempted to seek out Helen and ask for her support but she had faithfully promised the distraught Gill that she would confide in no-one. She got into bed, then got out again and stood by the door to check that Gill's bed looked occupied. Satisfied that it would pass muster as long as no-one came far into the room, she was just slipping back into bed when she heard heavy footsteps outside. Heart thumping, she stood poised, the corner of the bedcover in her hand.

There was a loud, aggressive knock on the door. Sarah wanted to rush across and lean her weight against it but she was too frightened to move.

"Sarah. Sarah Hanley - are you in there?" came the unmistakable tones of the Lion.

The door was opened, but only enough for Miss Schreiber to put her large head through the crack.

"Sarah!" she repeated. Are you awake? There's a telephone call for you."

Sarah was so relieved that she forgot her awe of the Principal. She went across to the door, making a great show of rubbing her eyes and yawning. Miss Schreiber stood aside to let her out.

"Really, Sarah - this is too bad," she said.

For a moment Sarah thought that she meant she had discovered the hoax body in Gill's bed. But Miss Schreiber pulled the door closed and marched off, beckoning Sarah to follow. As she went, she continued her lecture.

"Changing rooms without informing anyone so I have to go traipsing about the dormitory wing looking for you ... not even bothering to report in to Matron so that when your poor mother telephones I am made to seem foolish .... "

She paused on the lower landing and allowed Sarah to catch up.

"I'm sorry, Miss Schreiber," she said meekly. "But I assumed Miss O'Grady would have told you ..."

Miss Schreiber looked even more annoyed.

"Save your explanations for later," she said peevishly. "Off you go now to my study and talk to your poor mother. She is very concerned."

Sarah ran down the last flight of stairs, noting that the Lion swung round and made off towards the Staff Quarters - almost gleefully she wondered if Miss O'Grady was in for a ticking off.

"Hello. Mother?" she said into the phone, perching herself on the edge of the massive desk.

"Oh Sarah -everything's just terrible here. Mary is so broken up. Jane's away working at some Holiday Camp for a few weeks. I'm so glad I came ... I'm afraid Jack is very ill .... pneumonia and other complications ... Mary hasn't left his side for twenty-four hours . Look - are you all right?"

"Oh, yes," said Sarah. "Everything is fine, Mother. Don't you worry about me. Just concentrate on helping Mary."

"I'll try, dear. She's sleeping now, I think. We are at the hospital. I must go. I'll telephone when - er - if there's any news. Goodbye for now."

Sarah put down the phone and gripped the edge of the desk. She gritted her teeth. She wanted to cry, to scream - even, perhaps, to laugh out loud. This must be what is meant by hysteria, she thought. How can I explain my situation? Who can I turn to? She thought of Fred March. She looked at the telephone. Oh no, she told herself.

What could I say to him? Hello, Fred, here's the girl who tried to seduce you a few hours ago, pretending to be so sophisticated. Now I'm in terrible trouble. I've helped a girl run away. I'm frightened to death of two of the tutors. I can't ask my mother to help because she's so involved with Cousin Mary and her sick husband. No - it all sounds so crazy.

She left the study, switching off the desk lamp and plunging Fernleigh Manor into gloom, relieved only by a shaft of moonlight through the fanlight of the front door. This was sufficient to guide Sarah back to the stairs which led to Gill's room. She went all the way on tiptoe, praying she would not meet the Lion.

Just before she entered Gill's room she strained her ears and was almost certain that she could hear the distant sound of angry voices. Inside she saw that Gill's bed remained convincingly made up to look as if it contained a sleeping figure. She slipped into the other bed, said a last prayer that she could avoid discovery of Gill's absence till as late as possible tomorrow - and then fell asleep.

CHAPTER TEN

Not surprisingly, after the most traumatic day of her life, Sarah slept fitfully, escaping from one nightmare to find herself enmeshed in another. The corridors of her mind swarmed with motorcycles, taxis, the twin faces of the Willard sisters superimposed on the contrasting bodies of Schreiber and O'Grady. Jeremy, smiling and holding out his arms as she felt herself racing towards the safety of his embrace only to fall down an unseen staircase. Gill, cycling furiously, pursued by the Punk ....

Several times between dreams Sarah was awake long enough to raise her head and look over towards the other bed, then, seeing it unchanged, fall back exhausted into tortured sleep. Yet when the Rising bell penetrated her subconscious she had to make a tremendous effort to pull herself out of her final fantasy. Maddeningly, that one left a sense of happier connotations but because of her abrupt awakening the actual content had slipped out of her memory.

She felt terribly hot and sticky and hurried off to the nearest bathroom to shower before the bell for breakfast. It was one of the larger ones - divided into four cubicles and someone was already splashing in curtained privacy. The splashing stopped and a voice said warily, "Is that you Helen?"

"Marjory?"

Sarah thought she recognised the voice of Helen's roommate,

The curtain was yanked back and indeed there stood Marjory, a towel clutched around her. Seeing Sarah her cross expression relaxed into a friendly grin. She tossed the towel on to the floor and sank back into her bubbles.

"Sarah!" she chuckled. "Helen said you were back, Come on - draw up a bath and make yourself at home."

Sarah modestly drew back the curtain of the adjoining bath space halfway and turned on the taps.

"Here - help yourself to my foam," said Marjory. "Catch!"

She flung an expensive-looking bottle across.

"I don't much care for the flavour myself but never look a gift-horse in the mouth, eh? I'm trying to use it up fast."

Sarah knew Marjory even less than she knew Helen - she felt rather peeved with Carol who had pronounced her disapproval of this girl too. "Birds of a feather!" she had warned. "Marjory dogs Helen's footsteps - she's another bad lot!"

It had not crossed Sarah's mind to question these vetoes. Since that first day when Carol had offered such refuge from the strain of her first encounter with the Lion, she had trusted her new friend implicitly - like an abandoned ducking following the first creature it encounters and adopts it as a Mother. But now she wondered - should she have mixed in more with other "sets" - joined in the gossip - that way she might have learned more about, and armed herself against, the mysterious sense of danger she felt around her at Fernleigh.

"My, but you are quiet," said Marjory. "Trouble at home?"

"No," said Sarah. "At least - well, yes."

"Thanks for the confidence. Remind me not to ask in future," said Marjory but in a good-humoured way,

"Sorry! What I mean is - we do have illness in the family but its a distant relative - not my mother."

"Oh, hecky thump! Sorry to hear that - what tough luck to have to come back and leave that delicious punk of yours ..."

Sarah scrubbed furiously at her clean knees - so - Helen had had a good laugh with Marjory about her confidences. Marjory appeared, stark naked, in Sarah's cubicle. She perched on the ugly little cork-topped stool.

"Is there anything we can do to help?" she asked.

She seemed to be genuinely sympathetic. Maybe they hadn't laughed at her after all.

"We would have taken up with you earlier, you know," Marjory went on.

She produced a packet of cigarettes from her sponge bag. She offered it to Sarah but did not press her to take one though she lit up herself.

"That's one of the reasons we didn't pursue you. You seemed so - innocent. We didn't think you'd stomach our naughty little ways though we'd seen some underlying sense of fun in you."

She hugged her knees, tossed back her head, eyes screwed up, mouth creased in an expert grasp of the cigarette. Sarah could not help admiring her lovely figure and her long, black shining hair. Her first drag thoroughly savoured, Marjory removed it to speak.

" ... and then, of course, you had Christmas guarding your every move."

The nickname they had given Carol was not pronounced with any affection.

"There would have been some talk about you two being so close if we hadn't all known about the Christmas's famous - ahem - friend."

Sarah brushed aside the reference to the possible misunderstanding of her relationship with Carol.

"Famous?" she asked.

"Oh yes - and absolutely ancient - a writer, no less - always on the telly - at least, he was - till she ruined his life ..."

"H - how do you mean?" Sarah was wide-eyed with astonished curiosity.

"Well, I must be fair - not his life - he must adore the girl - but his reputation's gone to pot - perhaps his whole career - it's been in the papers this week - didn't you see it?"

Sarah shook her head.

"They kept Christmas's name out - and the college. Somebody must have pulled a few strings - it's just the kind of thing the gutter press thrives on - Big Scandal at Business College. Marjory and I knew about it ages ago - we saw them out together - at a hôtel, no less ..."

"So - what's actually happened, then?" asked Sarah. "I mean - what did the papers say?"

"He's run off to Paris with her, it seems, to starve in a garret. Left his rich wife and dozens of babes at home - they live in Fernleigh Court - the twin of this place - across the park."

Sarah fell into a daydream about Carol. She realised now that she had known very little about her. She wondered just how she had met this old man and why she had allowed herself to break up his marriage. She speculated on what he looked like - was he older than Fred March - had he had the same effect on Carol as the first sight of Jeremy had had on her - ah, then one might begin to get a glimmer of how it could have happened - Carol must have been very much - she tasted the idea hesitantly - very much in love ....

Helen came in, yawning and blinking at the harsh electric light.

"Mornin' all," she said lazily. "Smoking again, Marge - you'll look fifty by the time you're twenty. Everything all right, Sarah? Is Gill OK?"

As she idly posed these questions she entered a close-curtained cubicle and they heard the water running. Marjory held out her hand for the bottle of bath essence and Sarah handed it over. She was curious when Marjory, still unashamedly naked, did not enter her friend's cubicle but simply stuck her arm through the gap in the plastic curtain.

"See you back at the ranch!" she said. And, to Sarah - "Coming?"

Sarah sprang out of the bath and made a pretence of fumbling for her towel so that she could turn her back on Marjory. Nevertheless when she had dried herself and pulled on her robe she turned to find Marjory still staring at her.

"Not bad. Not bad at all," she said between puffs.

She was clearly trying to finish the cigarette quickly before going out into the corridor.

"Hey, Helen, our little Sally's not at all bad looking - we should take her on you know - we really should."

"Sure," came Helen's voice. "Just what I was telling her last night. How about making a start this evening?"

"We'll go back to her place and discuss it, eh?" shouted Marjory, opening the door for Sarah.

She nodded at her to go out.

"You go ahead," she said. "I just want to make sure Helen's OK - she gets giddy sometimes in the steam."

Sarah remembered Gill and wondered what to do - she decided to take a chance and tell the other two. After all it must be half past eight. Gill would be on the first regular train in less than half an hour even if she hadn't found an alternative method of transport - and it would be such a relief to share the burden of the secret. Her mind made up she turned to see Miss O'Grady, looking awfully plain in a pink plastic shower cap, coming towards the bathroom. Sarah stepped back into the open doorway and said pointedly, "Are you coming, then, Marjory, to help me wake Gill?"

Marjory, semi-clothed in a brief thigh-length kimono, stepped out just as Miss O'Grady reached them. Her face stiffened. She stared icily at the tutor. Then she looked at the long-handled brush the woman was clutching - ludicrously, it was shaped like a mermaid.

"Helen's just had a dizzy spell," said Marjory.

Sarah thought she detected a warning - or even a threat - behind the words.

"She's OK now - she's just coming out."

Miss O'Grady glared back at Marjory. Ignoring Sarah completely she went on her way.

"Grrr!" Marjory was grinding her teeth. "One of these days ..."

She took Sarah's elbow and they crossed to Gill's room.

Marjory was not fooled for a second by the tricked-up bed. Sarah supposed she and Helen must have used this ruse many times. "Oi, oi!" she said, pulling back the cover, revealing the pillows. "What's all this, then!"

"Please, Marjory, don't tell ..." began Sarah.

"Look, luv," interrupted Marjory. "Christmas may have warned you off Helen and me - but whatever we are - and we are not, I admit, angels - but we are not sneaks either. Come on, Sally - you look worried sick - hey - you don't mind me calling you Sally, do you?"

"No, no - that's all right," said Sarah, who rather liked the informal sound of it. "Gill - she's run away - she didn't say why - she's gone to her aunt in the Lake District. She didn't say why!" she repeated emphatically.

"Didn't need to, poor kid," muttered Marjory and again her teeth were grinding in rage. "Look, kid, before Helen comes - I'll tell you something - she's not been well - she's had an - operation. Oh, what the heck! She's had an abortion. That's why she's at this lousy place and not at a decent school - "

She gave a sidelong look at Sarah.

"I guess we all have our reasons for settling for here," she said and her face was haunted by some private pain. "Well, to cut a long story short - the Lion and the Mouse - you know, Schreiber and O'Grady - they feel they've got a hold over her because of that - as for me - no, skip that - the point is - have they tried to bully you yet?"

Sarah shook her head. It seemed easier than searching her own conscience for a completely-defined answer.

"Well - don't worry - you're under my protection now and I know the way to handle their sort. I should!" she added bitterly. "So - if either of them gets out of hand - starts trying to take you over - just come straight to Aunty Marge ... oh, hello, Hel'."

Helen was staring at the empty bed.

"Close the door," said Marjory. "You'll never believe - our little Gillian's made off in the middle of the night."

"Good for her!" said Helen. "Didn't know she had the guts. Now - how can we keep it from the Lion?"

"Easy!" said Marjory. "We ask for a tray. Every day's a Sunday in the half-term hol."

On Sunday it was permitted to take toast back to the dormitories for friends who preferred a lie-in.

"Yes, Cook will co-operate. She tells me she gets double time for staying over the hols with us little handfuls," said Helen.

Sarah wondered why a girl from such a luxurious home should choose not to go there at half term. Then she recalled what Marjory had just told her and realised that Helen was probably not welcome at home just now - in disgrace, in fact.

"We'll make sure everyone sees us bringing the tray for Gill," said Marjory.

"What about lunch?" asked Sarah.

It was Helen's turn to have a bright idea.

"We sign her out. In fact we all sign out and say we're going on a picnic - er - to do some sketching."

....

Marjory tackled Cook straight away when they went into breakfast. There were only half a dozen other girls in the dining room and no sign of Miss Schreiber or Miss O'Grady.

"Mornin', Mrs Ogmore!" said Helen brightly. "Want any help?"

"If you like, luv," said the cook and sat down heavily on a kitchen stool. "Come through ..." she invited, pointing to the service door. Moments later, Marjory appeared on the kitchen side of the serving hatch.

"I'll do the eggs," she offered.

She leaned over the small counter.

"Whose for fried eggs?" she yelled.

Grateful cries of acceptance came back from the girls who had been gloomily staring into bowls of cornflakes. Mrs Ogmore settled her huge bulk more comfortably. Sarah watched, fascinated, as Marjory, obviously no stranger to this kitchen, assembled her tools and began cracking eggs into a huge black skillet. Helen, amused at Sarah's widening eyes, laughed.

"She often takes over in the hols," she explained. "She's a born cook - but don't ever let her hear you say so - her ambitions lie in other directions."

She gestured towards one of the unoccupied tables. The two of them sat down. Helen pushed up her hair at the back, making a temporary chignon of her reddish curls. Sarah found herself admiring female beauty for the second time that morning. But Helen hadn't at all the same kind of good looks as her friend. Marjory, with a flashing, gypsy-like appeal had at the same time a quality of - Sarah searched for the word - ladylikeness was the best she could come up with. Sarah remembered Carol mentioning something about her being adopted and, rather scathingly, that she lived on a Council Estate somewhere in the sticks. Now, Helen, with all her aristocratic connections, had a certain coarseness of feature - and with her hair up like that and a slight pout she could be a ... no, Sarah refused to pursue this thought. It was outside her experience like so many things she thought wistfully. And now Helen had met her gaze and was studying her in return.

"You ought to pluck your eyebrows, Sarah," she said.

A couple of plates, each boasting two fried eggs, tomato and fried bread were thrust in front of them.

"Call her Sally for goodness sake," said Marjory. "This OK for everybody?"

"Do you need any help!" asked Sarah timidly.

"No but maybe afterwards we can all help Mrs Ogmore - give her a hand with the clearing away. I'll load the dishwasher."

Her voice suddenly increased in volume and vitality.

"And, Sarah, Mrs Ogmore is getting the - toast - for - lazy - old - Gillian!"

Helen lightly touched Sarah's foot under the table. Unhurriedly Sarah looked to her left and saw that Miss O'Grady was in conversation with the girls at the other table.

Mrs Ogmore, primed and rehearsed by Marjory, leaned out of the hatchway.

"Oh, Miss Meeks and Miss Croft," she called. "I'll be getting on with your packed lunches then - and did you say Miss Porter and Miss Hanley are for the sketching trip, too?"

Then, pretending to have only just noticed Miss O'Grady she shouted across the room.

"Oh, good morning, Miss. Will you be having eggs this morning? Miss Croft's been giving me a hand and there's plenty left."

Miss O'Grady shook her head and sniffed. She approached the hatch.

"Has something been burned?" she said contemptuously. "I'll just have a tray of toast to take to my room. I have some letters to get on with. Shall I take Miss Porter's tray too?" she asked and looked directly at Sarah.

Sarah pushed back her chair. "No - I'm ready," she said.

Marjory pushed her back down.

"Nonsense," she said. "Miss O'Grady can have all this first batch and we'll do some fresh for Gill - then she can have a good rest - she deserves it!"

She glared at Miss O'Grady and to Sarah's surprise the older woman lowered her eyes, picked up the tray the bemused Mrs Ogmore passed out and hurried away.

Marjory sat down and lit a cigarette. She tossed the packet to Mrs Ogmore who took one and gazed in undisguised admiration at the "young lady" she would later fulsomely praise to her husband.

Sarah felt such relief that the plan had gone off so well she settled back to enjoy the cup of coffee Helen had brought her.

CHAPTER ELEVEN

Sarah strolled as casually as she could manage to the high wall. It was the boundary which separated Fernleigh Manor's grounds from those of Fernleigh Court. Shrubs and trees clothed the brick and she soon found a broad-branched oak that was easy to climb. Once level with the top of the wall she heaved herself on to it and found it was wide enough to sit on in relative comfort. She peered through the branches on the other side and could just make out the gables and chimneys of the Court. She unwrapped Mrs Ogmore's sandwiches and munched as she brooded.

Marjory and Helen had made a great performance of setting off with her on their seemingly innocent expedition. They all hoped no-one would observe their little group too closely and comment on there being three rather than four of them. The other two girls' sketch books now lay with Sarah's in front of her on the wall. The reckless pair had stolen out of college by the vegetable garden gate, tossing their packed lunches into the compost bin. They assured Sarah that they would sustain themselves with liquid refreshment - they had a prearranged meeting with their chaps in the local pub. Their intention was to arrange a proper outing for the evening including a date for the new member of their clique. Sarah was not at all happy about things moving so quickly. Her inclusion had got out of hand - especially as she had avoided these girls only partly out of deference to Carol's advice - she had actually intended to work hard at

Fernleigh rather than seek out fun-loving groups. It was one thing to gratefully accept their expert help in covering Gill's tracks but quite another to cope with the abrupt change of lifestyle they offered. She was wondering just how she could get out of it without appearing too ungracious. After pondering her way through three cheese and pickle sandwiches she plumped for the idea of pleading a blinding headache.

I'll probably have a real one by this evening, she decided. Especially if I'm to do three lots of sketches as an alibi.

1   She opened Helen's sketch book and realised immediately that she had no hope of matching the attractive little drawings of odd corners of the Academy gardens, cleverly chosen because they compensated in their charm for the ugliness of the building, glimpses of which were allowed only at the edges of the compositions. The best were some studies of old weathered brick walls with peaches and vines trained over them. Sarah had never suspected Helen of possessing such talent. Because she had shown no interest in Sarah's pet subject ... but no, Sarah chased that thought away - the word Literature conjured up a disagreeable vision of Miss O'Grady. She put down Helen's book and opened Marjory's.

My goodness - if Helen's work showed talent - this was nearer to genius. Totally different in style, her work was mainly portraits - many instantly recognisable as students of the Academy. A few pages too of vigorous, blackly-shaded likenesses of the Lion and the Mouse - the dark side of their characters simply screaming out of the page. The last two pictures of the women were almost vicious in interpretation - but without being mere caricatures - the faces seemed to be staring at the artist with unconcealed hatred in response to her own opinion of them.

Sarah shut the book with a snap as though afraid the subjects would escape from it and threaten her in reality. But then her curiosity overcame her fear and she reopened the book and turned further pages. The later drawings were more sympathetically executed - so sensitively indeed as to suggest that these people were all the more loved because of the hatred spent on the two tutors. Two faces constantly reappeared - both middle-aged men and like enough to be cousins if not brothers. Both were handsome but both looked troubled - almost tortured - in every study. And, after a few blank pages, appeared a rather touching self-portrait - the gypsy element played down, an uncharacteristic serious expression, a demure, high-necked blouse - was that how Marjory would like to be? Sarah closed the book more gently, feeling rather ashamed, as though she had been reading the other girl's private diary.

She looked down into the garden next door - and she was staring straight into the face of one of the male portraits she had seen in the book.

"Hello up there!" he said.

Though he was smiling Sarah recognised the deeply etched lines on his face that betrayed his more usual frown depicted in Marjory's likenesses.

"Who is it, Derek?" asked someone who was as yet hidden by the bushes she seemed to be pushing her way through.

Sarah felt faint. She had come up here to try to get a look at the house of the man Carol had ensnared. She had hoped for just a glimpse of his home to help her try to understand her friend's motivation a little better. She had wondered as she found her way to this far corner if they had held their trysts here - but she had never thought to seek out the fellow in the flesh. Yet surely this must be him - he had the look of an artistic person - or an actor or writer. But why would he be in Marjory's book - and why was he here now and not with Carol? Who on earth could this female be - must be the wife Carol had wronged - Sarah prepared herself to see a dowdy, drab little person to contrast with the lovely vivacious Carol.

Instead the woman who appeared was breathtakingly beautiful - her hair was silvery grey but her face was not disfigured by age - more a case of being - enriched. And there was a close likeness to Carol in her features.

"Goodness," said Derek. "We don't usually have such an awe-inspiring effect on young women, do we Verna?"

Sarah thought this remark in poor taste in the present circumstances. She recovered her wits and said coldly, "I'm sorry. I shouldn't be sitting on your wall. I was just going to sketch your house."

"What remarkable eyesight you young ladies of the Academy must have!" scoffed Derek - but not unkindly.

Verna shushed him and said, "Anyone confined in that ugly mausoleum would naturally prefer to draw the Court. Why don't you jump down this side, dear, and draw us from the lawn. Our house was built by the sister of Lady Harriet who lived in the Manor - our Honourable Lionel had much better taste,"

She seemed a warm, friendly person though Sarah was puzzled that she was not more careworn by her recent tragedy. Perhaps she was overjoyed to have her husband back - Sarah felt so embarrassed at knowing their intimate secrets she felt she could not possibly accept their invitation. And she was rather afraid of the blandly-smiling Derek, whose forehead was creased with the constant memory of some long misery. After all, he had betrayed at least two women. But the strongest reason for refusing was that Sarah knew herself to be no artist and could not risk her bluff being called.

"No thank you. I think I'll go back and sketch in the rose garden." She went hot all over as she was reminded of Gill's distressing experience there. In her confusion she began to elaborate.

"I - I'm better at flowers than buildings," she stammered As Verna and Derek began offering the Fernleigh Court flowers as her subjects she scrambled on to the branch of the oak. In her haste to get away she did not notice Marjory's sketch pad fall down on the far side.

The two strangers seemed to be calling after her but she still felt threatened and so made off at a run for the seclusion of the Academy summerhouse. There she spent the remainder of the afternoon, going over and over the events of today and yesterday -

giving herself the headache she had planned to feign. This was made worse when she discovered the loss of the drawing book - she could not think how she could confess to losing it - let alone to let on that it had probably been retrieved by one of Marjory's models. She could not bear to think of the consequences if Verna or Derek looked inside the book - and surely they would. People don't usually feel the need to respect the privacy of sketch books, as they might with personal diaries, do they - or do they? As Sarah dragged her feet back towards the house she suddenly realised that Derek was not necessarily Carol's lover - he could just as easily be the other man - the look-alike come to comfort the deserted wife of his relative. Before she could digest the implications of this Sarah was diverted by a new shock. On the gravel sweep in front of the steps a police car was parked.

....

For a wild moment Sarah thought about going round to the laters` window or begging entrance at the kitchen door but before she had a chance to make a move Miss Schreiber appeared at the front door with a policeman.

"Ah!" she said significantly as she spotted Sarah. "There you are, young lady!"

She gestured towards the officer as though glad to hand over this wayward student for handcuffing.

"Inspector Bloom would like a word." To him she said, "Would you like to come back to my study?"

"No thank you, Miss Schreiber. I'll talk to Miss Hanley out here, I think - if that's all right with you."

"As you wish," she replied coldly. "In that case I will go and see if they've put through my International call."

When she had gone the policeman put his hand lightly across Sarah's shoulders in a fatherly, confidential way and led her on to the lawn.

"Phew! What a dragon!" he whispered.

This unexpected touch of humanity from an official source had such an effect on Sarah's troubled spirits that she burst into tears.

"It's about Gill, isn't it?" she gasped in between the sobs.

The policeman continued to smile at her reassuringly and to mutter, "There, there," to comfort her. But a professional alertness was added to his manner. When Sarah had recovered a little he said, "Gill?"

"She's run away," confessed Sarah. "I knew - and I didn't tell - she asked me not to say anything - has she been caught?"

"No, Miss - Sarah, isn't it?" he said. "You say this Gill - that would be Gill ...?"

"Porter"

"HM - this Gill Porter ran away - and just when was that exactly?"

"Last night," said Sarah. "Where is she now?"

"That we don't know," he said, watching her intently. "In fact, I'm hoping you can help us find her."

"Oh!" Sarah was puzzled. "Then she's been - reported?"

"A bicycle was discovered this morning in Fernleigh Woods. And later we found a haversack," said Inspector Bloom. Again he was watching Sarah's face closely.

"In the woods!" Sarah was shocked. "But - she was making for the station."

"Oh, she was, was she? And why was that, Sarah?"

"To catch a train for the Lake District - where her aunt lives - but I think she was too late ..."

Sarah relapsed into silence, remembering the pathetic little figure pedalling off. After a few moments the policeman spoke again.

"Too late?"

"I don't think she could have got there in time for the last train. I thought she would sit in the waiting room till morning."

"And now see what your woolly thinking has done!".

The voice was hysterical. They had strolled towards the rose garden and Miss O'Grady, red-eyed with mascara smudges on her thin cheeks, loomed up from a bench.

"Now, Miss - O'Grady, isn't it - " said the Inspector. " - calm yourself. I'm sure Sarah here did not realise the danger involved."

"Danger?" Sarah was stupefied.

"Well, let's not look on the gloomy side just yet," he said. "Your friend seems however to have - disappeared."

"But - couldn't she be with her aunt?"

"I'm afraid not - not yet, anyway," he explained. "Your headmistress telephoned there and added to my enquiries about the bicycle it was realised that no-one here had seen her this morning and the haversack having been identified as hers - of course, she could still be on her way to the Lake District by some other method of transport - let's hope that is the case. Now Sarah, is there anything else you can tell me that might help us to find Gill - to make sure she is - safe,"

Sarah was looking beyond the policeman to where Siobhaan O'Grady stood glaring at her.

"Well ... " she began hesitantly. " ... she was very - low - when I came back from home."

"How do you mean - low?" he probed.

"Oh, sort of nervous - jumpy - I don't know ..."

Miss O'Grady interposed her body between them, nodded to the Inspector, drew him a little way off. She said something in a voice too quiet for Sarah's ears.

"Oh, I see," he responded. "Right - thank you, Miss. Well, Sarah ... "

He turned to the white-faced, trembling girl.

"You've had a bit of a shock - best go inside, eh? I'm sure Miss O'Grady will square it with Miss Schreiber if you go straight upstairs and rest."

Siobhaan O'Grady shot her a look of triumph which made Sarah's heart sink - what could she have told the Inspector? But grateful enough to get away Sarah entered the building. Fortunately the Lion's door was closed. At the top of the stairs the girls stood goggle-eyed, waiting for their fellow student.

"What's up?" cried one as Sarah pushed past.

"Why have they been searching your room?"

Sarah stopped, taken aback.

"My room?"

"Well - Gill's room."

Sarah hurried on up and saw that the door was wide open. Gill's bed was neatly made up, covers tucked over the mattress, no sheets - like they do in a hospital when a patient has left - one way or another. Again a wave of fear at the awful finality of such a gesture. So - poor, frightened Gill was to be expelled - at least, she was not expected back. This was confirmed when she looked in the cupboards. All Gill's belongings had been taken away. Even the book shelves were empty.

Sarah turned anxiously to her side of the room. Her stuff seemed to be all there - but the extra neatness of her things suggested that it could have been examined and then carefully replaced. The doorway was filled with curious faces.

"Please," said Sarah and fell back on her bed, exhausted. They backed out considerately and closed the door gently.

Sarah ignored the bell for tea but after the supper bell she rose and splashed her face with cold water from the small hand basin. She felt rested but still dreadfully anxious about Gill and, she was rather ashamed to admit to herself, about her own position in regard to the Authority of the school and of the Law.

A tap on the door startled her but before she could move Siobhaan O'Grady was inside the room and had firmly closed the door. She crossed over to Sarah's portable radio and switched it on. Pop music blared out and she turned up the volume even more. Then she swung round on Sarah and, catching her unawares, slapped her face - hard. Sarah gasped but she was young and strong and she reacted quickly to this, only the second act of violence ever perpetrated against her - she shoved the crazed woman away from her with as much force as she could muster. The woman's eyes flashed, her lips drew back over her teeth in a snarling sarcastic grimace. Breathing hard, she came towards Sarah. Sarah held out her arms to ward her off but Miss O'Grady who had always seemed small and frail knocked them away and stretching out her own long, thin arm, grasped Sarah's hair and dragged her across the room.

There was a loud knocking above the noise of the radio. The snarl on O'Grady's face turned into a fearful grimace. She let go of Sarah's hair and crossed over to the radio. She turned down the volume and croaked hoarsely . "Who is it?"

"Who is in there?" came an angry voice. It was the Lion.

....

The Lion soon despatched the Mouse. O'Grady slunk out of the room without a word. As she passed, her colleague murmured, "Fool! And today of all days ..."

Then she closed the door and stepped further into the room. She stared at Sarah who was clutching her aching head. In a syrupy voice she said, "My poor child. Whatever has been going on here?"

Sarah did not know how to answer. Surely the question was not seriously meant - surely the Lion must know that the Mouse was - mad. The Lion came closer.

"The other girls are all at supper," she stated.

What does she mean to imply by that, thought Sarah. That no help is near? Or that the others need never know that there is a maniac in the place as long as I agree to keep the secret? Shall I scream?

"Sit down, my dear," said Miss Schreiber. "You have a nasty bruise on your face. I'll bathe it."

She took a man- sized handkerchief out of her pocket and dampened it at the basin. Sarah backed off towards the window. She could feel her face stinging where the insanely-angry O'Grady had slapped it. And for what? Did she blame Sarah for Gillian's running away, for bringing the police to the school - for somehow interfering between her and Gill - for not responding as she should to the tutor's earlier offer of friendship?

"I've been assaulted," said Sarah. "My mother ..."

"... must not be worried with extra problems just now, surely, Sarah, must she?" interrupted the Principal. She dabbed gently at Sarah's cheek and murmured. "Oh, my poor Sarah..."

"Sarah - are you up here Sarah? Yoo-hoo .... Sally girl...."

Voices from the garden echoed the big woman's words. She stepped back, alarmed, as Sarah flung the window open wide and leaned out. Marjory and Helen were below. Sarah put a finger to her lips and shook her head in warning. They ducked out of sight behind the bicycle shed. Miss Schreiber was mopping her own head with the damp handkerchief. She sat down heavily on the bed as Sarah strode across to her dressing table, picked up her comb and tidied her tousled hair. Staring the quivering woman straight in her fleshy face she puffed a little powder over her damaged skin then turned to the mirror and daubed lipstick on her mouth. She seldom wore make-up and did not make a good job of it but it made her feel better. Indeed she felt light-headed and reckless.,

"Goodnight, Miss Schreiber," she said as she pulled on her coat. "See you when I see you ..."

She marched out of the room, along the corridor, down the two flights of stairs and boldly out of the front door. Once on the drive she broke into a run, turned the corner of the West Wing and joined Marjory and Helen by the shed.

"Come on," she said, to their astonishment. "Lead me to Doug's friend."

CHAPTER TWELVE

All the way to the station, Paula cradled Mary in her arms like a baby. Every now and then a noiseless sob, a tight little shudder, shook the body of the bemused widow. Paula wished Mary would let it out, cry, scream, allow the tears to flow. Usually so fussy about not crushing her clothes, Paula was totally unaware that they were both dishevelled. She so much wanted to take Mary straight back to the cottage but she had refused point blank.

"I must be at our 'ouse till the - funeral," pleaded the poor, shattered soul.

....

How ghastly had been Paula's first sight of her cousin at the hospital - the plump figure usually topped by a grinning face advertising her comfortable happy-go-lucky attitude, more often than not, humming or singing to herself now sat, lumpy, silent, shrunken - a poor, shabby, plain woman waiting at the door of the room where her Jack lay struggling for breath. She stared glassily at Paula but could not speak. Yet when the smart woman who had caused a stir of interest amongst staff and visitors sat down on the bench next to her the fat, middle-aged woman put out a hand and allowed Paula to envelope it in hers. They sat thus for an hour until Paula went to telephone the school. When she returned a white-coated doctor was standing in front of Mary. Her face was as white as his coat, her eyes stared more glassily than ever but there was no sign of tears.

She rose and said to Paula, "We'd best go 'ome now. 'E's gone."

"Don't you want to see him?" whispered Paula, gently stroking Mary's hand.

Mary sucked in her lips with a sharp intake of breath and shook her head emphatically.

"I'll call a taxi," said Paula. "You wait here."

The doctor walked to the telephones with her. He handed her a tiny box.

"A couple of sleeping pills for your ..."

"My cousin!" said Paula and felt acutely aware of her own shame at having kept Mary and Jack in the background of her life, denying by omission their blood ties.

She went back for Mary who was still standing as she had left her, outside the ward. As they drew level with the row of telephones Mary said, "Our Jane - shall you tell 'er for me?"
She opened a scuffed handbag which had been well past its best when Paula passed it on to her ten years before. She took out a crumpled piece of paper with a number scribbled on it. Paula propped Mary against a radiator for the woman felt ice-cold. She was soon finished.

"Jane is catching the next train," she said. "We'll go to the station and pick her up and then we can all go to the cottage. There's still time to catch the midnight connection."
But with the minimum of words, Mary made it clear that this plan would not do. The widow and family waited and mourned privately between death and burial in their own familiar surroundings. The neighbours must be received, the ordeal must be faced as working-class convention demanded. That way you only had to skim over

what was happening, not torture yourself with trying to work things out. Not yet ...

Paula wished fervently that it was Fred March she was dealing with as she asked the stony-faced driver to take them to the station to meet an unspecified train.

"I dunno," he said, sourly. "Will you want me to wait?"

Paula could well imagine Fred's reaction. She was sure he would have been as solicitous for Mary, a complete stranger but obviously in distress, as for herself.... her mind lingered for a moment on how she was taking it for granted how deeply concerned he would be for her. But he was so plainly a good person and after all it was no insult to be admired.

"Come on, Missus, make up your mind," said the disagreeable man.

Paula had never missed her little red Mini as much as she did now. In its first youth she had used it mainly for shopping and driving to the hairdresser's. Later, Tom had borrowed it more and more as he could not afford both petrol for his Rover and his own personal fuel. Then the Rover had gone altogether and he had practically taken over her car - when he was in a fit state to drive.

Suddenly Paula's intense contempt for the male sex returned and chased away any fond thoughts of Fred March. Ignoring the surly cab driver she turned and led Mary towards the town. She recalled a taxi rank a few blocks away in the High Street.

"'Ere! Wot's goin' on? A bookin's a bookin'!" the irate driver called after them.

Paula put her arms round Mary's shoulders as though to protect her from his abuse. She got a little satisfaction from glancing back to see the hospital porter burst out of the main door and reprimand the noisy individual.

"Not far to walk," she murmured to Mary who, though unprotesting, stumbled along heavily on her swollen, varicosed legs. They stood for a moment under the arch of the Hospital Gateway while Paula tried to orientate herself. Headlights spot lit the two women. The car braked, then swerved, turned in the entrance and drew up by them.

Paula blushed deeply as Fred March jumped out - as if he might read on her face signs that she had recently been thinking of him.

"Phew! What good timing!" he said, a little breathless with joy at recognising that, for whatever reason, Paula seemed glad to see him.

He looked from her to the disinterested figure of Mary and summed up the situation. He looked back at Paula and she confirmed his conclusions with a sad little nod. He spoke again, in a low voice this time.

"I came on the off chance," he explained. "I was off duty at nine and you'd told me the name of the hospital. It's only an hour and a half by road. I wondered if there were any way I could help."

1Paula was so glad now that she had relaxed her reserve in his taxi and told him about Jack and Mary.
"I'm - we're - so grateful, Mr March," she said. "Could you take us first to the station to pick up Mary's daughter?"

"Of course," he said, opening the door for Mary.

The other taxi driver drove out of the grounds. He screeched to a halt and down his window.

"Listen 'ere, Missus ..." he threatened.

Fred straightened up from helping Mary inside. Paula felt the thrill she had never thought to feel, that she had given up hope of waiting for, that she had pretended did wound not exist, as she sheltered behind Fred's broad back. The other man hastily drove off, subdued by the flash of anger in Fred, outraged that anyone should dare to speak to Paula that way. Fred turned to Paula and looked at her not

hiding his indignation on her behalf.

"Has he been giving you trouble?" he demanded.

Paula could not at first answer. His clear blue eyes looking into hers,

full of concern, were too much. She had a powerful impulse to step

forward just a few centimetres and lean into his body, wait for his

arms to enclose her. On his part Fred was begging silently to be

allowed to hold her to his chest and stroke her gleaming hair.

Behind them, Mary made a choked little sound, another

attempt to hold herself in check, not to give away to her

overwhelming grief. Paula climbed in beside her, saying, "I did book

his taxi by phone but he was so rude ..."

Fred closed the door and went round to his own seat.

"I'd a good mind to look up the ..." he muttered.

....

At the station Fred gestured to Paula to stay in the car. She told him

where Jane was coming from and he went in alone to check the train

times.

"Just arriving now," he said, through the window, a few minutes later.

"You stay here, Mary," said Paula, but again Mary stubbornly refused. They went on to the almost deserted platform, Fred seeing to the platform tickets. As the train came into view, Mary's legs seemed to give way and she and Paula, clasping each other, sank on to a rather slimy bench. Fred stood a little way off.

The train drew in with the usual squeaking and banging. Only a handful of passengers emerged. Jane, looking terrified, jumped down and hurried to her mother. Mary stood up.

"'E's gone, luv," she said, and at last the tears came.

Small-framed Jane dropped her suitcase and took her mother in her arms and somehow the overweight, blousy woman found herself supported. Jane looked at Paula over her mother's heaving shoulders, "About an hour ago," confirmed Paula. "Come .... Mary ... "

But Mary clung fast to her Jane.

Fred stepped forward and picked up the case. Jane and Paula between them coaxed the sobbing woman out of the station. Several people looked curiously towards the group then quickly averted their eyes in respect for the privacy of grief.

Mary half lay across the back seat, one woolly-gloved hand pressed into her mouth in a vain attempt to control herself, the other arm sprawled across Jane's chest - as though she were the child seeking comfort of the parent. While Fred stowed away the case, Paula got into the front passenger seat. He could hardly contain his pleasure at discovering her by his side.

"Home?" he asked.

The word had a similar effect on both of them - all it could imply - their common longing to be driving back to a shared house - a cosy fire, a simple supper - a warm bed.

He did not start the car immediately. He put his hand on top of Paula's as it lay on her knee. She found herself melting from breast to ankle, mostly around belly and thighs. She closed her eyes in the rapture of the sensation.

Is this my reward for helping Mary? she wondered and reminded of the poor soul in the back she said aloud, "Mary wants us to go to her house in Brook Street."

Content in the knowledge that she need not rearrange her face to talk to this man, she added, "... near the gasworks."

As they drove he occasionally touched her knee as he changed gear and they stole quick looks at each other from time to time - not smiling, but infinitely tender .... an urgency, too, had crept into their eyes - a mutual hunger.

Paula no longer felt the slight hurt from Mary's turning away from her once Jane had appeared. It was, she acknowledged, a relief to have the burden of responsibility lifted slightly. In Brook Street Paula pointed out the grimy little house and jumped out quickly when the car stopped. She and Jane bundled Mary inside while Fred retrieved Jane's meagre piece of luggage. He set it down just inside the room which gave directly on to the pavement. There was an awkward silence. They were all still standing. Then Mary spotted Jack's pipe on the mantel-shelf. She seized it, gazed at it, then turned to Jane. Her face crumpled. Jane gently led her off up the narrow stairs.

Fred did not move closer to Paula but he spoke hoarsely.
"It's the same for you, isn't it?"
Paula's voice, too, was husky.
"Yes, my dear, the same ..."

"What are we to do?" asked the young, strong, virile man - and he pointed to the ceiling.

"I find I'm not needed here after all," said Paula?. "You can drive me .... home."

Fred took deep breaths. His love flamed up in him and the power of it crossed the small room with its threadbare, none too clean carpet, hardly a romantic setting, to the glowing, newly-awakened woman opposite. He made as if to move towards her.

"Wait," she said. "Wait in the car - darling."

When Jane came down, Paula embraced her and the two cried together for a few minutes. Then Paula held her away and looked into her eyes.

"You're a tower of strength to your mother," she said.

She was reminded of Sarah. What would her own daughter think of her mother's shameful behaviour - after all her jokes about Fred. She pushed the thought away. She would not be denied this chance. Deep inside her she knew it was right.

"Will you be all right?" she asked Jane, who had begin to rummage round for her father's bits and pieces and gather them together. Jane looked questioningly at her.

"If I leave you, I mean," said Paula.

"Oh, yes - yes, Paula, of course, I'd forgotten - Sarah's home for half-term, isn't she? And not used to being on her own. Yes - yes, you go. I'll get in touch about the - funeral."

Paula let the misunderstanding about Sarah ride - it was better for everyone that way. She handed over the sleeping pills and kissed the girl once more. Then she went out to Fred.

1...

They did not speak a word till they were clear of the town. Then he said, "I'll stop here," and drew in to what at first looked like a lay-by but turned out to be a farm gateway. He took her in his arms and their first kiss was so blissful that Paula felt she would faint from the joy of it. She leaned her head back and Fred rained quicker, lighter kisses on her throat.

"Sweetheart. Angel," he murmured. She cupped his face in her hands and kissed his full sensuous mouth.

"Darling," she said. "This is crazy. I'm so much older than ..."

He stopped her lips with his and ran his hand along her body as though to deny any shortcomings.

"You - are - beautiful." he said. "And you are all I want, have ever wanted ..."

He looked deeply into her eyes for a long moment, then bent his head and, gently opening her blouse, kissed her shapely bosom. Then he briskly re-buttoned her, pulled her jacket into place, turned away and started the engine. He threw back his handsome head and laughed and Paula gloried in his strength, his vigour.

"Why skulk in a car like silly teenagers?" he shouted. "We've got a home to go to ..."

"Yes, oh yes," she cried, matching his merry abandoned mood. "But drive quickly, my love."

....

There was one moment of solemnity. Fred discreetly parked the taxi behind the cottage in the empty doorless barn which was the nearest the property could claim as a garage. Then, as they stood together in the porch while Paula found the keys, he put his hand on her arm.

"Paula," he said.

"Yes?"

"Do you truly want me?"

"I do, Fred, truly," she said.

He sighed.

"Then I'm yours - and , for me, Paula, that means for ever."

....

...........................After a night of passion Paula had never dreamed
of attaining, they woke to the same soft, country sounds Sarah had
enjoyed a couple of days before. They were still locked in each
other's arms. Fred playfully rubbed her nose with his.

"We'd have found each other, eventually you know - even if I'd been
an Eskimo," he said.

Paula stirred, luxuriating in his embrace - and desire was re-aroused.

"You're even more lovely in daylight," he said, afterwards,
lying on one elbow, watching as she pulled on a bathrobe. Paula
smiled and opened the bedroom door. Seeing the door opposite she
was reminded again of Sarah.

"Darling," she said, over her shoulder as she set off down the stairs,
"Remember I've got a daughter of seventeen."

A frown clouded his face. Sarah, he thought grimly, I hope I don't
have to face her too soon ....

****

****

It was less than two weeks later when he saw Sarah. His taxi had been booked by telephone from a roadhouse ten miles away. He'd pointed out that there were more conveniently-placed firms to use. The male voice assured him that he had been highly recommended. "I've got your card, old man." he said and put down the receiver.

Outside the flashy club, buried in a remote part of the countryside and seemingly based on the roadhouses of the American movies, a girl was being supported by two middle-aged men as she threw up into the bushes. One of her companions wiped splashes of vomit from his jacket with a handkerchief and looked with disgust at the sick girl. She turned and hurled abuse at him, calling him a fat, squeamish pig. It was then that Fred recognised Sarah .....

CHAPTER THIRTEEN

Sarah was taken aback when she saw the boys waiting for them at the end of the drive. She looked back at Fernleigh Manor, in two minds whether to go back, collect her belongings and leave the place for good. She had thrown in her lot with Marjory and Helen in a spirit of revenge but could she live up to her impulsive decision? Could she strike back at a world where up till now she had tried to live harmlessly, obediently, - even humbly? She still felt resentment that her innocent existence had been repaid with a day of puzzling, violent, passionate encounters with members of both sexes. She looked across the road where Marjory and Helen were already sprawling all over Phil and Doug as they leaned up against the dirty chassis of an old banger of a car. It seemed that the owner, still ensconced in the driving seat, must be Sarah's blind date. Her heart lurched as she remembered Jeremy sitting proudly at the wheel of his beloved vintage car. This new boy lit up a cigarette and revealed a sallow, greasy complexion, coarse features and a day's growth of beard. Sarah took a step backwards, repelled.

"Come on. Sarah - don't keep Reg waiting!" called Helen, barely turning from her escort, round whose neck she was inelegantly draped.

Sarah thought of Gill who had tried to escape and would probably suffer the disgrace of expulsion without summoning enough nerve to say one word in her own defence. Was she herself stronger? Did she believe fervently enough in the evil of that woman back at the school to be able to convince her own mother, let alone the police? Reminded of where Paula was right this minute she was even less sure of how to approach her, so involved with another family's problems, when her own story would probably sound so vague .... And what if Jeremy got to hear about it? Like an unexpected wave on a calm sea, Sarah's desperate hysterical recklessness returned to overwhelm her. She crossed the road and was bundled into the car with nothing resembling a polite introduction. Just a few jibes on the lines of "Reg is a right drag but he's got the transport" and "Sal's fresh out of the nunnery but she's got possibilities, you'll see." There was much squeezing and pinching from the boys in the back seat and one of them leaned over to playfully bite Sarah's ear.

1   Sitting beside Reg was hardly inspiring. He chain smoked and gave not one glance in Sarah's direction. This was not because

he was a careful driver: he screeched round the bends, braked hard at the last possible moment at every corner and seemed rather unfamiliar with the gears. Sarah began to suspect sinister connotations in the phrase "Reg has the transport". She had supposed it to mean he owned the car or had at least borrowed it from his father. Now she wondered exactly how he had acquired it and how recently.

Recognising some landmarks she realised they were driving in the general direction of her home. If only... she mused, and squeezed her eyes shut to prevent tears forming .... if only she was simply being driven back to the cottage by Jeremy - or even in Fred's taxi - and Mother was waiting there, everything made bright and comfortable to welcome her as she had found it last time .

"Where are we going?" she asked timidly.

"Gorblimey - it can speak!" said Doug, thrusting his grinning face forward,

"The Blue Moon Roadhouse," supplied Helen, who seemed to have become aware of Sarah's tension. She pulled Doug back.

"You live out this way somewhere, don't you?" she said to Sarah.

For a moment, Sarah thought she was about to suggest to Reg that they deliver Sarah back home after all. But Marjory put her oar in.

"Here, Sarah, before we arrive and get all hot and high and - involved...." - she made the word suggestive by putting her face where Doug's had been and winking lasciviously - " ... are you going to fill us in on what exactly has been going on in our absence at the Mausoleum?"

"Yes," agreed Helen, her concern for Sarah's nervousness forgotten. "I hardly gathered a thing from your babbling as we rushed down the drive to our - hmmm - lover boys."

She ran her hand along Doug's thigh and this time it was he who pulled her back.

"Gill Porter's bike has been found by the police," said Sarah patiently though she would have much preferred not to think about it all again. "In the woods."

There were hoots of laughter from the two boys in the back.

"Oh, do shut up!" said Marjory. "Go on, Sal ..."

"Schreiber and O'Grady seem very upset about her going off like that," said Sarah lamely.

"Well, ducks, they 'ave lorst a paying guest, 'aven't they?" said Phil.

"No," said Sarah. "It's more than that."

"I'll say it is," murmured Marjory angrily. "Go on - what did they say exactly - to you?"

"O'Grady came to my room and - assaulted me like a - madwoman," whispered Sarah, hoarse with the disagreeable memory.

Marjory shot forward again.

"The cow!" she breathed,

Helen put a hand on Sarah's shoulder.

"Poor kid!" she said.

"Then Schreiber came in and acted - funny " added Sarah. "She seemed to be asking me not to let anyone know about O'Grady's attack. Actually, for her, she was quite - gentle - almost humble."

"Weird!" said Helen

"And she might even get away with it - again!" muttered Marjory.

But now the car had screamed to a halt in front of a gaudy building, brilliantly lit, with music blaring out and, above the entrance, a revolving neon moon of a disagreeable electric blue. Reg switched off the engine, alighted from the car and strode off up the steps, apparently without the slightest thought of opening Sarah's door or helping her out. The others stumbled out of the back, falling over each other and laughing loudly. Sarah struggled with the catch, then realised that it must be jammed. She slid over to the driving seat, swinging her legs high to avoid the gear stick. Phil and Doug ceased their horse play and stood back gaping in admiration.

"Get a look at those pins!" said Phil.

"Wot a luvverley pair!" said Doug.

Sarah pulled down her skirt and got out, blushing.

"I told you she had possibilities," said Marjory - who seemed a bit peeved especially when the two boys took an arm each and escorted Sarah up the steps with an exaggerated gallantry, leaving the two other girls to their own devices.

"Here, Reg!" called Doug as they entered the Reception Area. "Take a look at this."

He bent down and before Sarah realised what he was up to, flipped up her skirt to reveal her long, shapely legs as far as the thighs. Even the dour Reg seemed impressed. The suggestion of a smile appeared on his face and he retraced his steps. He snapped his hand down on Doug's arm, causing him to let go Sarah's clothing and a howl of pain to burst from his lips.

"I fort you knew she wus mine - O.K.?" said Reg in an unattractive guttural voice. Sarah saw that he was tall - a head and shoulders above Doug and Phil. Doug made no protest. He swaggered off with an enforced air of unconcern to cover his loss of face.

"Give us yer coat!" said Reg ungraciously.

Sarah shrugged it off and handed it over. He tossed it on the counter of the cloakroom alcove and the attendant handed him a ticket. This he pocketed, and Sarah saw the action as a symbol of his already avowed ownership. She felt a faint stirring of amusement. She remembered with enjoyment the surprised look on Doug's face as Reg's huge hand came thwacking down on his arm. She thought back to Marjory's look of chagrin as the boys admired her new friend's legs. It almost made up for any previous embarrassment. She saw the group now, clustered at the bar, eyeing her - the boys still openly appreciative, seeing beyond her rather school girlish party frock - the girls plainly jealous of her fresh, good looks. She realised for the first time how pleasant it can feel to be admired. Her spirits lifted: she would try to get all she could out of this new experience, enjoy any adventure it held out for her - after all, nothing could be more traumatic than the happenings of the past few days.

A glass was thrust into her hand and she was led through the tightly-packed crowd of young people to a table near the rock group on the small stage, fronted by the usual aggressive, wild-eyed, hollow-cheeked guitarist. The room was very hot and she drank thirstily. The drink was new to her - rather sweet but not unpleasant. The disco lights flashed on and off, Helen and Doug got up to dance. Marjory and Phil launched into a bright, flippant exchange of jokes and retorts - everyone seemed happy - her spirits rose even further.

"Wanna dance?" asked Reg.

Sarah looked at the dancers though she had a little trouble focussing - was it the heat or the lights that seemed to make the room go round and round ...

"I don't know if - I - can ..." she said - it was with some difficulty she got out these simple words.

Reg snatched up her glass and smelled the contents.

"Swine!" he shouted at Phil and dashed the contents of the amber liquid in his face.

"'Ere - wot's up?" gasped Phil.

"Yes - what's going on?" demanded Marjory, mopping up Phil's saturated shirt.

"Get 'er a lemonade or summink," ordered Reg, and Phil wasted no time rushing to obey the stronger youth.

He's really quite kind in his own uncouth way, thought Sarah, hastily divining through a very woolly head, that Reg was indignant on her behalf, that the others had played a dirty trick on him, through her, in revenge for being made to look foolish. It seemed to have backfired and now Reg was showing a real concern for her. He leaned close.

"Go to t'lavvy - try 'n sick it up," he said quietly.

damp from dabbing at Phil. She pressed it over Sarah's hot face.

"That was rotten," she said. "But it wasn't Phil's idea, I'm sure - it was that sod Doug - Sarah could not help shuddering at the indelicate way he put it but at the same time she realised that intense nausea was also making her feel trembly.

"Come on," said Marjory. "I'll go with you ..."

She held Sarah's shoulders as she vomited into the none-too-clean lavatory pan. She led her over to the wash basin and wrung out her own handkerchief, still and then he made sure he was out of the way when it had its effect. Here - use my lipstick - it'll suit you."

Marjory's jealousy seemed to have evaporated. She's looking after me just as she does Helen, thought Sarah, beginning to feel better.

"You'll be all right now," said Marjory. "Just sip at the lemonade - don't gulp it - then I'll get you a shandy - that'll put some go into you without knocking you out. And you should have a snack - I bet your stomach is empty - that's the worst thing to do."

Sarah took her advice gratefully and in half an hour when Reg again suggested dancing, she stood up eagerly. She had been enjoying the music since her head had cleared - the only dancing she had so far tried, apart from her ballet classes - had been a waltz or a foxtrot in drawing rooms of school friends cleared for birthday parties and watched over by staid and starchy mothers done up like duchesses. However she had a good sense of rhythm and had quickly seen that there were no set steps or moves to be learned in this jolly, uninhibited type of dancing.

In no time at all it was plain that Sarah had taken to jiving like the proverbial duck to water. By the end of the evening, other couples were standing back to make a space round her and applauding as she danced - Reg was a negative performer, he conceded one or two movements as a foil to her twisting and swaying. Neither Doug nor Phil had suggested taking a turn with Sarah though both were much better dancers than Reg and though she wondered briefly if it would be more exciting to try other partners she felt she owed something to Reg for his previous gallantry.

By the time they left the club Sarah was truly inebriated - but not with alcohol - she had stuck to lemonade - no, it was the dancing that had intensified her mood of abandoned enjoyment - she was drunk with the newly-discovered exquisite sensation of it.

She leaned back on the torn leather seat - Reg had managed finally to wrench the stubborn door open and usher her in. She closed her eyes and spent the entire return journey reliving the glorious moments when she had been one with the beat of the bass, felt her body responding to the rhythm and saw the admiration of the other dancers.

In no time at all, it seemed, they were at the gates of Fernleigh Manor. They all spilled out of the car. Doug and Helen immediately disappeared into the copse on the left of the entrance, Phil and Marjory plunged less urgently, but obviously following a set routine, into the bushes on the right. As Sarah gazed after them, wide-eyed, Reg grasped her arm and nudged her back to the car - and into the back.

There was no hint of the gentleman now as he thrust up her skirt and lunged his heavy body on top of her.

"Christ! he cried in an agony of lust - and pressed his thighs hard against hers.

So, thought Sarah bitterly, her jubilant mood destroyed in moments - so, another act of violence - and it was no concern for my health and well-being which prompted his rescue back at the club - he just wanted to ensure I was fit for ....ugh - this.

The car was small, Reg was big. He moved slightly to try to find a more comfortable position for his over long limbs. Sarah rolled from under him, dived out of the door - fortunately this one erred on the other side in being loosely closed - shot across the road and raced up the drive.

"Little cow! Teasing bitch!" she heard him call. Then the sound of the engine.

Sarah leaped across the ditch and hid behind a tree, afraid he was going to pursue her in the grounds. But the diminishing roar of the old banger, followed by shouts of indignation and running footsteps revealed that he was driving away without his companions. Sarah slid to the ground, her back to the oak, and peering round its bulk laughed hysterically at the sight of Doug and Phil, clutching at their disarranged clothing, chasing after the car. It squealed to a halt to let them, still protesting, scramble on board and then zoomed off again.

Minutes later, Marjory and Helen appeared from their separate love nests. Both looked annoyed but when they heard Sarah's breathless bursts of description they too began to giggle. "Oh my - if you could have seen Doug, hopping along with one shoe in his hand - hopping at sixty miles an hour, mind you - and the terror on Phil's face as he buttoned his jacket up all wrong and patted his pockets to see if he'd lost his wallet." The three of them sat all of a heap, giving themselves over to hilarious laughter.

At last Marjory calmed herself.

"Cripes, Sal," she said. "Do you realise that the reason you had such a good view of that comedy was because of this brilliant moonlight. Come on, my children, we must pull ourselves together if we are to get ourselves into the old window, undetected."

"Didn't you fancy Reg at all?" asked Helen, pulling her clothes into shape and patting her hair back into place.

She seemed genuinely puzzled that Sarah should not have wished to end the evening in the traditional way.

"I suppose he is a bit of a creep - but anyway you seem to be able to take care of yourself ..."

"Ye-es sir!" agreed Marjory, thoughtfully. "Hey, Helen, what's the name of that other chap Doug used to drag around with him - he'd be better for Sal next time."

Sarah jumped back across the ditch and, humming one of the tunes demanded most often by the fans of tonight's jazz group, did a few practice steps down the middle of the drive.

"Don't bother," she said as the other two took her firmly by the arms and led her towards the grim building. "I'll just to along with the four of you - and see what - or who - turns up."

"She's right," said Helen. "With her looks and talents she'll soon find her own partners."

As Sarah fell asleep that night on a mattress the other two had dragged in between their beds, her last thought was of Paula. From the depth of her newly-acquired knowledge of the companionship of the opposite sex - and even though the advantages had been for her outweighed by the disadvantages in this particular instance - she dragged out the sleepy thought, I wish mother could find a nice man ....

CHAPTER FOURTEEN

11

For three blissful days Paula and Fred indulged themselves in a veritable honeymoon at the cottage. Each night, Fred discreetly hid the taxi in the barn and tried not to return between bookings during the day, except sometimes for lunch. Both of them found this rationing of their time together a terrible hardship. Both were ravenously hungry for each other's companionship - they had so much time to make up, getting to know each other. Besides which, Paula had developed an appetite for food - she occupied the lonely hours of waiting for her lover by preparing delicious meals for him - and delighted in sharing them.

Then they had a narrow escape. The Willard sisters called on Paula a few minutes after Fred had driven off. Paula was just about to clear away the remnants of their midday meal when she heard the knock. Assuming that Fred had returned, and immediately roused and ready for his embrace, she dashed along the narrow hall and flung open the door, delight all over her face, lips pouted for his kiss.

"Why, Paula!" gasped Miss Isobel. "You look so - well!"

"Wasn't that Fred March's taxi we saw in the lane?" asked Miss Fanny. "You haven't got guests have you? Or - has Sarah been sent home?"

"Come in," said Paula and was conscious of the open kitchen door, revealing the lunch table with its two plates. She rather clumsily interposed herself between the door and the visitors, ushered them into the front room and kicked the kitchen door shut.

"Do sit down," she said with a quick glance around to see if Fred had left any telltale belongings. "I'll make some coffee."

"No, no, dear - not for us," said Isobel. "We just came about the trouble - at Fernleigh."

Paula felt sick with fear. She had had a few twinges of guilt the past few days about being so happy while Mary was suffering so terribly - but she had not given a thought to her daughter.

"Trouble!" she echoed.

"Yes - look - it's in the paper!"

Miss Fanny handed Paula a newspaper folded back at a column headlined MYSTERIOUS DISAPPEARANCE OF PRIVATE COLLEGE PUPIL. Her heart sank. She let the newspaper fall to the floor.

"You look dizzy," cried Fanny, stepping forward to support the half-fainting Paula.

"I'll get some water," said Isobel, making for the kitchen.

Her sharp eyes quickly took in the details: table laid daintily for two, a bottle of wine half empty - and her keen mind jumped to a fairly accurate conclusion. She smiled to herself but managed to put on a sober enough expression as she held the glass to Paula's lips. "Now," she said. "To put your mind at rest, my dear - it's not Sarah they are looking for - oh, aren't we a couple of silly old fools giving you such a shock - but we thought you knew, you see - I'm sure Sarah's quite all right."

Paula face had more colour now and Isobel watched the glow return to her eyes - though not quite the look of rapture that had caught her by surprise when Paula had opened the door so eagerly. She retrieved the crumpled news-sheet and read out key phrases.

"Gillian Porter - last seen Wednesday evening - bicycle said to belong to the eighteen year old student - discovered Fernleigh Woods Thursday morning - haversack found later near the same spot - identified as the missing girl's property - parents in Africa - Aunt in Lake District has been informed - one of the lesser-known private Secretarial schools for young ladies, the Academy ...."

"How awful!" said Paula. "I must telephone Sarah at once."

"Of course," said Miss Fanny. "And - if there's anything we can do .... But now we'll leave you in peace to get in touch with Sarah."

Her sister was signalling that they must leave straight away. But Fanny lingered.

"We also were wondering how is your poor, dear - cousin?"

"Oh, I'm so sorry," said Paula. "I should have let you know. Jack died. Mary was shattered, of course, but ..."

She hesitated, not wishing to lie but aware of all the connotations of her being back so soon, yet having confined herself to the cottage.

"Her daughter is with her. I - I - left them to grieve together."

"Yes, dear, of course - that was very understanding of you," said Fanny, putting a hand on Paula's arm. Paula caught Isobel's eye as she stood waiting in the doorway. She could not miss the twinkle of mischief. Fanny went on.

"And you must have done your own share of mourning, here, all alone for three days."

Isobel let Fanny go past her and then turned back to Paula.

"I don't know exactly what you have been doing for three days, Paula," she said. "But it's certainly done wonders for you. you look about twenty-five."

Waving and winking, she joined her sister in the lane.

Paula examined her face in the mirror.

It's true, she thought. I can't hide my happiness. What are people going to think? What does Isobel make of it?

She went into the living room and dialled the Fernleigh Academy number. Miss Schreiber answered and, usually so gushing to Paula, she sounded now decidedly cool. Paula attributed this to worry about the missing girl. She expressed her sympathy and then asked if Sarah was upset. There was silence at first.

Then the deep voice said - "Ah - Sarah hasn't been in touch, then?"

"No," said Paula. "You see, she thinks I'm still at my cousin's - she doesn't know I'm back home."

Reminded of the three idyllic, stolen days, Paula's legs felt weak.

Right on cue she heard a car draw into the lane, then recognised that

it had turned round the side of the house. Fred - she could not wait to

be in his arms .... Miss Schreiber was still talking and Paula had

missed most of what she had said.

" .... may have to SEND THE GIRLS HOME .... REPORTERS

DOGGING THEM .... PALAVER WILL DIE DOWN

EVENTUALLY ..... TOO MUCH BEING MADE OF IT ..... LET

YOU KNOW OFFICIALLY .... SPEAK TO THE GOVERNORS

..."

The phone was slammed down abruptly. Paula had picked up one

vital piece of information but she pushed it to the back of her mind

as she heard Fred's footsteps coming to the kitchen door. She ran

into the little sun-lounge to greet him. She flung herself at him and

pulled him down on to the floor amongst some cushions she had

been re-covering. Pins stuck into them, their clothes and hair were

full of cotton fluff but the urgency of their need for each other made

them unaware of such details.

Afterwards, Fred lifted a strand of Paula's hair and whispered into her ear. "You're as bad as I am, darlin' - you need it all the time, don't you?"

"Only with you, my love," whispered Paula, pushing back his shirt with her slender hand. She kissed his bare shoulder and gloried in the feel of his strong, muscular chest against her firm, rekindled breasts.

"And to think," he teased her, "that I only came back for my booking list ..."

Paula pulled away from him.

"Fred, sweetheart - you very nearly bumped into my visitors."

Fred stood up and pulled her to her feet.

"High time we had a talk, my love," he said. "We haven't really had time for a serious discussion, I know - we get within two metres of each other and - boom - the magnet pulls us together."

He deliberately placed himself on the far side of her sewing machine - creating a barrier.

"But now, my Paula, we've got to make time ...."

Paula sat down.

"Yes," she agreed, but despondently. "We must talk."

"Marry me - now - tomorrow - next week ..." said Fred, beaming down on her, full of confidence.

"Sarah's being sent home," she blurted out, with something approaching a sob. She had been trying to hold back the dreaded information gleaned from Miss Schreiber - from herself as well as him.

Fred came round and took her in his arms.

"Now, now. darling," he soothed. "Why so upset? What's happened?"

"There's some sort of trouble at the Academy - oh, I'm sure Sarah's not involved. Another girl, though, is missing - the police are involved - it's in the papers - the Press are still snooping about - the headmistress seem to be thinking of closing the school down for a while."

"O.K." said Fred. "It's a shame. A bad business by the sound of it. But it can't affect us, can it?"

"But, Fred - I can't spring ...er ...us ... on Sarah like that. I must build up to it carefully."

Fred stepped away. He looked at Paula but now there was misery on his face.

"Look at me," he commanded.

Paula obeyed.

"It's not just Sarah, is it? You're not sure, are you?"

She shook her head, denying his assumption. He was unconvinced.

"These visitors you mentioned - the Willard sisters?"

This time Paula nodded assent. Words were beyond her for the time being.

"You know, I was sorely tempted to lean out of the cab window and shout to them - I wanted to yell I adore Paula! We devour each other night and day!"

Paula looked horrified. Fred came close again and stared into her eyes.

"Didn't you feel tempted to tell them how you feel about me?" he asked, probing her face with his clear eyes. "Don't you want to scream out your joy to the whole world?"

He stepped back.

"Or are you ashamed?" he asked.

"Please Fred," said Paula, reaching for his hand. "Don't force me to - do anything yet - give me time - there's Sarah - and Mary ...."

Her voice faded. Fred went through to the kitchen and found his list. His face was grim when he returned.

"Goodbye, Paula," he said and went out into the garden, closing the door gently - but with a finality that made Paula's heart thump. She sat alone with her thoughts for a half hour, then went to phone Mary.

CHAPTER FIFTEEN

Fred was thankful for a full list of bookings but eventually, about nine o'clock he had a breathing space. He sat alone in the small office, hardly more than a shed, attached to the house of his partner with whom he also lodged. He ached to ring up Paula and ask for her forgiveness. But for what, he reflected - for loving her too much. Surely he had not imagined the strength of her feelings for him: and it was not just physical attraction on either side. That side of it was marvellous, sure it was. But when Davy and Chris had made suggestive remarks about his not having slept in his own bed recently, his first reaction had been to want to tick them off for sullying his love with cheap humour. It was too precious to him. It was not just a casual affair. But he had respected Paula's reputation and had kept his reply noncommittal.

"You know how it is."

He kept his tone light to match their banter.

"You were young once yourselves."

As Davy and Chris were exactly his own age they took the joke in good part and there was more nudge-nudge, wink-wink. Fred wondered how Paula would take to Chris - she was a bit untidy and happy-go-lucky but kind-hearted with it. Nor dare he let his mind dwell on Chris's opinion of his taking Paula as his mistress - the two women must already have a nodding acquaintance as Chris ran the village store which, as in many small rural communities, was also Post Office, wool shop, toy shop. Fred seemed to recall seeing Paula in there once buying reels of cotton.

Outside, in what had originally been the blacksmith's forge, sat two old but still serviceable Rovers, mostly used for weddings and funerals of the more modest kind. Fred and Davy had been friends since their schooldays in the East End. Fred had been best man at Davy's wedding to Chris. Then the factory where the two young men had started their working lives together, first as mechanics, later as drivers, had closed down. Chris and Davy had warmly welcomed Fred, and the small amount of capital he offered to chip in from his redundancy money, into this business they had bought, miles away from their native London. His contribution had allowed them to add a modern taxi to the set up and now their combined efforts were showing results.

Before Fred had declared himself to Paula he had lain abed, plotting and scheming how to accelerate their fortune so that he could present himself to her as a man of means. At that time he had hardly been able to believe that he would ever have the courage to approach her - until that night at the hospital when, joy of joys, he read the message of her mutual feelings and - he was committed for life.

Now Fred put his head in his hands.

You fool! he thought. How could you have believed it would last for ever? There were always too many problems. Background. Sarah. Age.

The latter was no real problem as far as he was concerned - he really meant it when he told her it made no difference, meant absolutely nothing to him. And as for the first - he would have tried so hard to improve himself for her if she had shown any signs of being put off by his lack of gentility.

He picked up the evening paper to try to dodge painful thoughts of what might have been. He was shocked to read the full account of Gill's disappearance from Sarah's school. Then he realised that it was a marvellous excuse to ring Paula. But before he could do so, the phone bleeped.

A slurred voice summoned him to the Blue Moon Roadhouse. Oh yes, the voice assured him, it must be Dawson and March Car Hire - the young lady had insisted. Wearily Fred entered the call in the log and went out to the taxi. Dejectedly he drove off through the villages in the direction marked out on his map. He had a little trouble towards the end of the journey as he was in unfamiliar territory. But at last - there was the roadhouse. And there was Sarah.

How on earth had she got herself into such a state, Fred asked himself as he sprang out of the cab. And what sort of place was this Fernleigh, already front page news for losing one student, yet allowing others to roam so far afield ...

****

****

Sarah was eager to go dancing again. She nagged Marjory and Helen all through the following day. But they were rather taken by the reporters who continually gave Schreiber and O'Grady the slip and managed to corner students to give 'unofficial' interviews.

"It's killingly funny to see the old Lion's face when she turns a corner and finds yet another eager young chap furiously taking notes while one of her 'well-protected' young ladies spills the beans," chortled Marjory. "I mean to say, look at all the business she'll lose when Parents cotton on to the fact that just about anybody can get in here!"

"Or out!" commented Helen.

"Yes," agreed Sarah. "Out. As I was saying - when are we going out?"

At last she wore down their resistance.

"It'll have to be a bike ride this time," said Marjory. "We can hardly get in touch with Reg, can we?"

She glared at Sarah who after all was responsible for ruining their chances of using that particular transport again.

"And I shan't be able to face Doug for days," said Helen.

"Well, that's not such a bad thing," snapped Marjory.

"I know, I know," said Helen. "Leave it, Marge, please ..."

"Bikes it is then, as soon after supper as we can decently manage," said Marjory. "We don't want to push Schreiber too hard - she might crack too soon. I want to see her suffer as long as poss. You can use Carol's cycle, Sarah, seeing as she obviously has no need for it and as you were such a close friend of hers."

So it was that Sarah added a new scenario to her increasing list. She was introduced to the modern equivalent of a Barn Dance - a Village Hall Hop. It was Saturday and it seemed there were many such events in the locality but Marjory and Helen in their wisdom chose a spot quite a distance from Fernleigh Village. The fruits of the local hamlet had not gone untasted by the daredevil pair but they did not fancy being questioned ad nauseum as well-known fugitives from the Academy about recent events. Anyway, some of the more stuffy adults in attendance might well have been tempted to report them to the school.

As predicted, Sarah had no difficulty in finding partners in this unfamiliar environment. On the whole they were shy young country lads, farm workers mainly.

"Bumpkins, if ever I saw one," slavered Helen, practically rubbing her hands with glee at the sight of their bulging muscles.

But after the first thrill of pleasure at the ease of wresting attention away from the rather red-faced, plump local females, Sarah became bored. She wondered why her mother had been so adamantly against rural seasonal festivities. She had hinted scornfully at unwelcome memories of Harvest suppers, Christmas Dances, Easter picnics in her own teenage years but she could never be drawn out - she would assume a dreamy, faraway expression backed up with a frown of determination not to relive that period. Some of the people into whose elevated social sphere Paula had pushed her daughter, had country properties and had invited Sarah to stay, promising 'local colour' when visiting Parish 'do's'. Paula had warned Sarah to refuse - assuring her that such functions were always just an excuse for rowdy vulgarity. Sarah suspected strange complexities behind Paula's judgement: hence her curiosity about this evening had been all the more heightened. But looking across to the refreshment table

Sarah could at this moment see a vicar, cast in the same inoffensive mould as Cyril, being fussed over by several respectable-looking ladies more or less interchangeable with the Willard sisters. What harm could Mother have anticipated at a set up such as this, wondered Sarah. She's all mixed up about her snobbishness - so anxious to know the right people she doesn't always recognise them when she sees them. I wonder what made her like that ....

Poor Sarah had as yet not an inkling of the complexity of Paula's make-up - of the dreadful struggle she had experienced when she was Sarah's age, fighting her way out of a background in which she felt so out of place, so suffocated, so frustrated. About the dreams she had of marrying an aristocrat - of becoming a lady of the manor. About her yearning to discover that she was a changeling - that in fact she had blue blood coursing through her veins, throbbing and pressurising her to achieve her rightful place in society.

Neither could Sarah have imagined in a lifetime of Sundays that at this precise moment her strict, unbending, high-principled parent was leaning voluptuously over a young taxi driver, running her hand the full length of his muscular, naked body. Something innately sensual in the mother had, however been passed on to the daughter because now, the music being changed to a slow, sultry blues - albeit from a record on an ancient audio system - Sarah was dancing in a way these people never would have thought to see in their little thatch-roofed Hall. She was oblivious of her partner, a tall, raw-nosed young man with trousers two inches too short. She was also unaware of the other dancers - most of whom were giving up all pretence of moving to the music in order to watch this slim young stranger undulating in perfect complement to the beat and rhythm. She had forgotten for a few blissful moments all the recent events which had turned her life upside down.

"Salome!" whispered the vicar.

"A disgrace!" said his wife. "Get them to change the record, Herbert. One of those jitterbug things - they're more wholesome."

Marjory, standing near enough to overhear, would have normally been eager to share her amusement with Helen. But she had earlier seen that young lady sneak outside into the field which served as forecourt, overflow refreshment area and smoking room. She had been leading by the hand the only real tough character present this evening. He had arrived, sporting a shapeless Army-surplus parka, anxious to be recognised as a bona fide Mod. Now Marjory thought she could hear the revving-up of his motor-scooter. She strode into the cloakroom and grabbed all three of their coats. Marching into the middle of the room she took Sarah unceremoniously by the hand and led her away, ignoring the protests of the enraptured audience. "Sorry, folks. We must love you and leave you," she announced. "Another time, eh?"

"Wh- wh- what?" said Sarah who might have been mistaken for a drug addict, so disorientated was she by her own response to the music. Outside, Marjory bundled her into her coat and pushed her over to the bicycles.

"C'mon, love, shape yourself" she pleaded. "I've got to manage two bikes and we've got to try to catch up with that crazy loon, Helen - oh, lordy, what a hope ..."

"Where is Helen?" asked Sarah, revived somewhat by the wind blowing in her face as they pedalled off, Marjory inexpertly guiding Helen's bike at the side of her own machine. They made slow progress as Marjory lost control of one or the other machine time after time and wobbled to a standstill to regain her balance. Finally, with a grunt of disgust, she hid Helen's bike behind a hedge, vaguely noting its position in the hope of retrieving it later.

Ten minutes afterwards she wished she had persevered with the two machines. As they rounded a sharp bend in a lane so overhung by beeches as to give the unnerving impression of being in an endless tunnel, they came upon a distressing sight. Helen was tearing her way out of the undergrowth. She tripped and fell into the ditch. Marjory threw down her bicycle and ran to her friend. "What's happened?" she demanded.

1Helen could not speak. She was in an awful state, clothes torn, face and hands scratched and bleeding.
"That young bum ..." said Marjory threateningly.

"No, no - get me home quick - I'll explain later ...."

"Wait here with her," Marjory commanded Sarah. "I'll go back for the bike."

Sarah took Helen's coat which she had hung over her handlebars and wrapped it round the trembling girl. Helen shrank back into the shadow of the wood.

"Hide your bike," she whispered.

Thoroughly puzzled, Sarah nevertheless fetched the bicycle into the depths of the ditch and kicked dead leaves over it. Then she put her arms round Helen and was about to speak.

"Shhh!" warned Helen.

Sarah listened intently. Yes - someone was walking through the trees behind the girls. Walking stealthily - searching? Now and then a branch snapped, leaves rustled. At one point Sarah could have sworn that she felt, rather than heard, heavy breathing very close. She squeezed her knuckles into her mouth to keep from coughing - or screaming. Then, weirdly, they heard sharper footsteps on the lane way ahead - receding, getting fainter and fainter - going away.

"Who do you think ..." whispered Sarah.

Helen's hands were clasped over her chest, as though trying to quiet her thumping heart.

"Here comes Marjory," she said. "Let's get out of here."

The girls were so shaken by their unsought adventure they were almost reckless about climbing in to school. Once in their room, however, Sarah and Marjory turned to Helen for some explanation. She was looking in the mirror at a bruise on her cheek.

"The little sod!" she said, dabbing at it with damp cotton wool. "Just 'cos I said he was no good ..."

She turned defiantly to Marjory.

"Well - he wasn't!" she reiterated.

For the first time Sarah wondered just how promiscuous Helen was. She had only half-listened to the hints and sexual allusions between the two and, without examining her own thoughts too deeply, had accepted it as exaggerated boasting, partly to impress her. But maybe after all - she listened now more intently though she could not decide whether certain knowledge of how far they went with boys would affect her opinion of them.

"He whammed me in the face and then raced off on that stupid scooter, abandoning me to goodness only knows what ..."

Marjory shook her head reproachfully.

"I've told you to always stick close," she reminded her friend.

"I know, I know . Don't worry - in future ...."

She began to splash her face from the basin. Marjory passed her a towel.

"Listen you two - I'm more worried than ever about Gill now," said Helen, drying herself and then trying to shake the twigs from her hair.

"I was just sitting there, fuming, wondering what to do next when I suddenly knew - ugh, it was awful - I was being watched. And I've a strong feeling that - whoever it was - had been there all the time - watching - er - us ..."

"Yuk!" said Marjory.

"I was frozen to the spot with fear at first," admitted Helen. "There were funny movements - as though an animal were arching its back, pawing the ground - preparing to pounce on its prey. Then there was deep breathing."

"Are you sure it wasn't an animal?" asked Marjory.

"No, no!" said Sarah. "I heard it too - I'm sure it was a man."

"Or woman ..." said Helen drily. "Or - maniac. Listen you two - I'm scared - for Gill - for us. Let's lay low for a while."

"Ought we to tell the police?" ventured Sarah.

"What are you saying?"

Marjory was impatient.

"Well, it's just, maybe it might help them find Gill."

"Look, love," said Marjory, more kindly. "If they're going to find Gill, they'll find her. no point in us stirring up trouble. Look - I agree with Helen - we'll tease old O'Grady by making a big show of obeying all the rules and voluntarily working in the Library - that should cramp her style. Then when we've got the screaming hab-jabs with the place, we'll take a quiet stroll down to the pub - you'd be surprised what fun you can have at our local hostelry, Sarah - eh, Helen?"

The pact agreed, they climbed into bed and were soon sleeping. Sarah's dreams were full of music and dancing, bicycles and bears, punctuated by disquietingly-real scenes of her mother arguing fiercely with Cyril.

....

Two nights later Helen had sufficiently recovered from her fright and was restless and bored. The trio slipped out at eight and made their way to the inn. It was not far so they went on foot, armed with heavy torches. They turned right at the gate and chose the busier, though slightly longer, of the two routes to the village. They did not fancy the lane through the woods.

Sarah was disappointed with the pub. There was no music and most of the clientele seemed ancient. The landlord welcomed the two older girls warmly. He raised his eyes at Sarah.

"Your friend old enough to be in here?" he asked - but he was joking.

"Three shandies, Harry," said Marjory. "Anybody interesting in the other bar?"

"I'd stick to the Snug," said Harry and nodded his head in warning towards the opposite end where a screen partially cut off the Cocktail Lounge.

Sarah peered round it and to her amazement recognised a huge figure humped over a table by the window as Miss Schreiber. Marjory pulled at Sarah, gesturing for her to follow them into a tiny room at the end. She grinned viciously at Sarah's astonished face. "It makes it more exciting knowing she's in there," she said. Sarah could not explain that it was not merely the sight of the headmistress which had shocked her. Sitting with her was the woman she had seen and talked to in the grounds of Fernleigh Court, the writer's wife, supposedly wronged by Carol. The two women were clasping hands across the marble-topped table. A handshake on a bargain of some sort? A gesture of friendship - or were they related? Sarah's attention was diverted by noticing that Helen and Marjory had begun a bold flirtation with two middle-aged men who had swaggered in from the Car Park where they had left a sleek, expensive vehicle.

Those two are no better than .... But again, Sarah could not put into words what she suspected of Helen and Marjory.

A glass was thrust in her hand by one of the men. She sipped gingerly, not wishing to repeat the experience on the first night out with her friends. It was rather strong but quite pleasant with a touch of bitterness. She saw Marjory nudge Helen. Defiantly she took a deeper draught.

"What's your name, beautiful?" asked the man who had provided the round. "I'm Roger."

"Sally," said Sarah, tossing back her hair. She studied Roger. He was nondescript. Smallish, thinning hair, his suit was expensive looking but did little to enhance his rotund figure.

"What am I doing here when I could be somewhere else - dancing?" Sarah did not realise she was speaking her thoughts aloud.

"Come on then, Sally, what are we waiting for?" Roger responded eagerly. "I've got the Jag outside. Where shall we go?"

Her bluff called, Sarah blurted out, "The Blue Moon?"

"Anything Sally wants, Roger can give ... " he boasted.

He stood up, holding the door open for Sarah. As she rose, she felt a little unsteady.

Not again, idiot, she reproached herself but then she was aware only of laughter, of people crowding her, of being bundled into an extremely comfortable car where she landed in a heap with Marjory and Roger's friend. Helen, in front, was leaning on Roger's shoulder as he drove, singing at the top of his unmelodious voice. Marjory whispered to Sarah, with a hint of spite.

"I can't keep on saving you, Sal - this time it's all up to you."

....

The evening passed in a whirl. From time to time, Sarah danced - but there was no modern group tonight   - just a dreary little trio playing desultory fox-trots. Roger seemed happy enough to smooch around the floor with Sarah, as long as there was copious drinking in between. Sarah began to feel ill - not like the sudden nausea she had felt before but a dragging, pounding sensation in her head, echoed in the depths of her stomach and a weakness in her legs. Finally she slumped over the table.

"She's passed out," said Marjory contemptuously.

Helen and Len had disappeared.

"Find your friend!" ordered Marjory. "And get us home. Pronto!"

"Wher-sh-home?" slurred Roger.

"Fernleigh Academy - our School," announced Marjory evenly

watching for the effect,

Roger sat up, suddenly alert.

"Did you say - school?" he said, disconcerted. "You're - school girls!

Look, I - er - there's not a lot of petrol in the old tank - I'd better get

you a taxi."

"Taxi," murmured Sarah. "Fred March - I've got his card."

She fumbled in her handbag and produced it. Roger grabbed it from

her.

"He's gone to pieces, thinking we're - under age," chuckled Marjory.

"Daft old pig!"

"Fred March'll come ..." murmured Sarah from the depths of her

stupor.

"Oh, lordy, Sal - pull yourself together," said Marjory. "I'll go find

Helen."

Roger returned and began to heave Sarah up from the table,

"Fresh air ..." he muttered.

He staggered to the door, Sarah inelegantly flopping over him. He tried to sum up enough dignity to stare down the giggling waitresses. As they continued unsteadily through the foyer, Len staggered out of the Gents cloakroom.

"That Helen!" he commented, slapping his friend on the back. "Some girl, eh?"

"Yeah," snarled Roger, suddenly sober. "GIRL is right - do you realise that the whole shower are schoolgirls - from some private school in that village - Fernleigh, wasn't it? Wish I'd never set eyes on that damned pub ..."

"Fernleigh?" said Len, pulling himself together as best he could. "That's the place that's in the news, isn't it? It's a college, not a school," he added without much conviction that this made a huge difference to the unpleasantness of the situation.

"Whatever ..." snarled Roger. "Help me get 'em out of here. I've got a taxi coming."

As the fresh air hit her, Sarah was sick. The two men hurried her over to some shrubs and Len at least had the decency to support her as she vomited. Sarah could not appreciate this small touch of

gallantry - she felt degraded as saw Roger wipe at his blue suit in
disgust.

"You fat squeamish pig!" she screamed, unconsciously echoing
Marjory's words.

Caught in Fred's headlights, Sarah was a sorry sight, screaming and
bawling like a fish wife.

Fred jumped out and, taking her from Len without giving the
two men a second glance, he helped her into the cab. Marjory and
Helen appeared from nowhere and after an appreciative look at Fred,
they clambered in with Sarah.

"Just look at that pair of eejits!" said Marjory as the taxi swerved
past Roger and Len, standing like a pair of rolling skittles, trying to
right themselves.

"What's all this about?" asked Fred.

Marjory and Helen looked at each other. They were not accustomed
to such a tone from drivers of hired vehicles. But this Fred - he was
some handsome guy.

"We've sneaked out of college," lisped Helen, putting on an air of
innocence.

"It's terribly grim there at the moment," added Marjory. "What with the police and reporters and all."

Fred glanced at Sarah.

"What's wrong with Sarah?" he asked.

Marjory and Helen exchanged glances.

"She's - just been a bit upset," said Marjory. "About her friend's disappearance - you must have seen it in the papers."

"Do you make a habit of sneaking out?" asked Fred.

"All the time, honey," said Helen, leaning forward. "You just name the time and the place."

"Turn left here!" interrupted Marjory who had noted Fred's disgusted reaction to Helen's advances.

"Perhaps Sarah should go straight home?" suggested Fred.

Marjory caught something in his voice which disquieted her, made her intensely jealous.

"Nonsense!" she said. "Do you want her to get expelled?"

Then, following her instincts, she added sarcastically, "That would be some comfort to her mother, wouldn't it"

Fred said nothing. There was something about this young woman he did not trust and he felt the need to be extra discreet. He dropped them at the gate and even accepted a tip from Helen though Roger had thrust a ten pound note into his hand already.

He watched Helen and Marjory frog-march the still-limp Sarah up the drive. He drove away but he was uneasy. He recalled Sarah's face, too heavily made-up, a new coarseness in her voice. He felt torn. He was tempted to punish Paula for the hours of misery she had caused him. He could easily ring her and inform her how mistaken she had been about the purity of her daughter. At the same time he longed to protect her from such knowledge - and comfort her - and hold her in his arms. He put his foot down on the accelerator and raced to the village. He stopped off briefly at his office to log the ride. Then he drove round to the cottage.

Paula was waiting for him at the door, alerted by the so welcome sound of his engine. She held out her arms and they sank to the floor, Paula cradling her lover to her breast as he sobbed, "Please don't send me away ..."

"Forgive me ..." she whispered into his hair. "We'll work something out - I can't bear to lose you."

"Anything you say, my darling," murmured Fred, pressing his lips to her bosom.

"Come," said Paula, gently pulling him to his feet. "Let's go to bed."

CHAPTER SIXTEEN

Jane and Mary were glad of Paula's support at the funeral. Closeted

together in the tiny house for nearly a week they had shared their

grief, for the most part silently. There were no words to express their

loss and the family had been so close-knit they had long been used to

communicating in other ways. A glance, a touch on the arm, a slow

shaking of the head. As well as missing her father for his own sake,

his good nature and ever-grinning attitude to life, Jane missed the

light-hearted banter between her parents - as good as a couple of

comics on a stage, they had their own peculiar jokes, references to

shared experiences - that needed only the smallest clues and hints,

family catch-phrases to revive amusing memories. She also sorely

missed her mother's singing as she went haphazardly about her

chores. Now Mary sat in Jack's chair for hours at a time, silently

staring into the fireplace.

Paula swept into this doleful scene on the morning of the funeral and decided that changes would have to be made.

"Jane, when are you going back to work?" she asked with a directness that was intentionally cruel in order to be kind.

Jane looked at Mary, slumped in the shabby wing chair, barely aware of Paula's arrival.

"How can I?" she asked.

Paula knelt on the dusty rug in front of Mary. She took hold of her hands.

"Mary," she said gently. "I could do with some company at the cottage. How about coming back with me after the .... tonight."

Mary stared at her vacantly.

Oh God, prayed Paula silently. Help me to get through. Don't let me weaken. It's bad enough having to ask Fred to stay away ...

Then Mary spoke.

"How kind you've always been our Paula," she said, dejectedly. "Our Jack and me - why ever did you bother yourself with folk like us?"

"I don't know what you mean," lied Paula. "You're family. And you're my friend. You've helped me often enough - let me look after you now. And there's your Jane. She must pick up the threads of her life."

"All right," said Mary. "Now I suppose I must get ready for ..."

"Come on, I'll give you a hand," said Paula, helping her up and noting with a pang how much greyer her hair had become in just a few days.

Paula shared their car but again it was Jane to whom Mary turned at this sublimely-painful moment. She stared at the hearse in front, at the coffin with its single wreath of blue flowers - Jack's favourite colour. She clasped Jane's hand.

"Is that our Dad in there, our Jane?"

"No, Mam," said Jane, cradling her mother in her arms. "That's not our Dad - he's here in our hearts."

Paula stifled a sob. She determined to do as much for this little family as her meagre sources would allow. Maybe Sarah need not have the skiing holiday this year .....

The ordeal of the service was followed by a poignant moment in the churchyard when Mary stepped up to the gaping grave and spoke clearly.

"Goodbye, me duck," she said. At that moment and during the tedious ham tea afterwards for the neighbours, Paula was pierced with guilt over her past attitude to her family. She reflected too on her most recent display of selfishness - her love affair. Fred had insisted on coming to fetch her that evening - how would he react to her bringing Mary along?

Jane left first, visibly relieved to be returning to the normal world of work, knowing she could hand over the burden of her mother's suffering to someone else.

"I'll never be able to repay you," she said to Paula, who had slipped a five pound note into the girl's hand. Paula knew she was not referring to the money.

At six Fred arrived and Paula could sense him struggling to hide the love in his eyes as he played the part of cab driver. It was difficult for her to remain calm in his presence, particularly as Mary seemed suddenly more alert. Nothing like her old jovial self, of course, but she did begin to bustle about checking doors and windows and helping with the packing of her few, miserable garments. Paula made a mental note that she must run up a couple of new dresses for Mary.

While the widow went up for a last look round - Paula knew this meant a last look into the shoe box unde her bed where she had stowed away Jack's pipe and watch and a few other knickknacks - Fred seized the opportunity to pull Paula to him. He kissed her but it was not his usual passionate embrace with its lingering promise of renewed rapture. A lighter, yet nonetheless pleasing brush of the lips - then he said - "I've missed you."

"After twelve hours," she teased.

Then, more seriously, "Fred - I hope you understand that as I've invited Mary to stay at the cottage ...."

He put his finger on her lips.

"Hush! What do you think I'm made of - ice?" he said. "I won't butt in. For one thing I don't think Mary needs to see other people in love just now."

Paula gasped. The comparison between their relationship and that of Jack and Mary shocked her. Yet of course those two had been in love. Plump down-at-heel Mary and skinny, long-nosed Jack may not have made a glamorous couple but in the eyes of the world their union was more acceptable than that of a middle-aged woman, no matter how smart, with a young, virile man like Fred.

"It'll probably make me ill," whispered Fred. "Maybe we can arrange ... no ... I wouldn't dream of barging in at a time like this."

He sprang away as he heard Mary coming downstairs. Paula marvelled anew at his kindness, his unselfish thoughtfulness. He really is something special, she decided.

Briskly she ushered Mary out to the taxi, feeling a rush of optimism about her own future.

"Do you think our Jane will be all right?" said Mary as they left the town where not so long ago Mary had felt her whole world safe and secure round her.

"Yes - she's a good, sensible girl," soothed Paula. "We have nothing to complain about where our daughters are concerned - they're both good girls - in their different ways."

....

How little Paula could have dreamt that the ways of Sarah and Jane were soon to clash.

Sarah was disenchanted with her first experience of a pub crawl, as Marjory called it, the next morning. She woke with a blinding headache and a revival of the nausea of the night before.

"Oh-oh-oh - I much prefer dancing to drinking," she moaned while Marjory mixed her a hangover cure from ingredients coaxed out of Matron and Mrs Ogden.

"Showing off to an audience is what you like," said Helen.

"No!" denied Sarah. "... at least - I suppose I don't mind people watching - but it's the feel of the music I love - the rhythm - the movement - can we go to another real jazz session?"

"We -ell," said Marjory. "There's usually something good on the Coast over the weekend. We could get in touch with Doug and Phil."

"Not Reg .... " pleaded Sarah.

Helen and Marjory laughed.

"OK OK Who else do we know with a car - or we could hitch." Helen seemed enthusiastic.

"Hitch!" exclaimed Sarah.

"It's safe enough with three," said Marjory.

"Mmm - some of those rough-tough lorry drivers," remembered Helen, dreamily.

"We'll want to be arriving before midnight," warned Marjory sarcastically.

....

On Saturday afternoon the three escapees made for the main road and Helen began at once to demonstrate some well-tried techniques for attracting the attention of passing motorists. At first, Marjory and Sarah kept a low profile, ducking behind a tree while Helen thumbed down the vehicles. But after two or three tries - aborted when the drivers saw that the attractive young girl had two companions with her - they changed tactics. Brazenly they strolled along arm-in-arm, singing at the tops of their voices and pretending indifference to the traffic. A huge tanker drew to a halt. The driver looked old enough to be one of their fathers.

"Goin' far?" he asked.

"The coast?" ventured Marjory.

"Jump in - plenty of room," he invited.

Helen hauled herself up but Sarah was rather daunted at the height of the cab from the ground and needed all the assistance she could get -

Marjory pushing from behind, Helen pulling in front. Marjory clambered in after her and slammed the door.

"'Avin' a night out?" chuckled the driver.

"We're looking for some action," said Helen. "You local?"

"No, luv - from London. But you shouldn't 'ave no trouble findin' some fun."

His tone, as far as Sarah could judge still seemed paternal but Marjory was scowling and Helen seemed restless. She fidgeted, making Sarah uncomfortable.

"What load have you got?" she asked.

"Milk, luv - you thirsty?" he joked.

"No room in the back then?" asked Helen. "It's a bit crowded in here."

Marjory leaned over and said, across Sarah, "How long do you reckon - you are heading for Bridgethorpe, I presume."

"'Baht 'arf an 'our, luv," he replied but he was glancing sideways at Helen. "Mmmm - let's see - there's a transport caff just inside the town - only five minutes walk from the front - that do you?"

"Fine," said Marjory. "By the way - are those your kiddies in the photograph?"

He shuffled on his seat, embarrassed.

"Me first grandchildren - twins," he admitted.

Helen cut in.

"You must have married young."

He beamed his appreciation of her flattery.

In the forecourt of the café, Marjory jumped down quickly and helped Sarah out. Helen lingered, finally allowing the driver to assist her down his side.

"Like a coffee?" he offered as Marjory and Sarah came round the front of the enormous vehicle.

"No thanks," said Marjory. "We'll be off. Come on Sarah - Helen?"

"You go on," said Helen. "I'll catch up later."

"Helen!" thundered Marjory.

"I just fancy a coffee," said Helen defiantly.

Sarah followed Marjory into the High Street but she could not resist looking back. Helen and the driver had made no move to go inside. They were still standing by the huge front wheel - standing very close to each other.

As they walked along the narrow street of the little holiday town, breathing in the ozone. Sarah ventured to quiz Marjory about Helen.

"What is it with her?" she began.

"Leave it!" warned Marjory. "I'm not in the mood."

Her mood lightened however a moment later as a fleet of motorcycles roared past, the riders shouting and waving.

"Looks as though there's plenty going on tonight," she said. "Come on - it must be this way."

....

If the first dance had excited Sarah, this one thrilled her through and through. The sides of the room were so crowded they had to literally force their way through. The music was deafening but the beat stirred Sarah so that she began tapping the air in front of her, clicking her fingers, swaying from the knees.

"We'll dance together at first," said Marjory, elbowing a space. This state of affairs was short-lived. Two young fellows infiltrated themselves between the two girls and matched their movements to their easily-acquired partners. Sarah hardly had time to draw breath as each record ended before another unceremonious touch on her arm announced that yet another stranger had laid claim to her. Sometimes they had the grace to add "OK?"

Dance after dance - soon Sarah was as intoxicated with the dancing as she had been with spirits plied from the bar.
Only this is much nicer, she thought.
She tossed back her hair and rejoiced at being alive and here at this moment in time.

She had been vaguely aware that many of her partners wore black leather trousers and she assumed they were motorcyclists. But this passing thought did not prepare her for the shock of recognition when the next fellow took her arm - it was the punk, the boy who had nearly run her down and later attacked her in the half-finished café. She was in half a mind to turn away and seek out Marjory and Helen, whom she had a moment before spotted in deep conversation on the edge of the crowd. But looking again she could see that they were involved in furious argument. Her second impulse was to slap the young man's ugly face. But then she became aware that he was dancing so much better than any of her previous partners - they had at best been foils for her. This boy, gaunt-faced and with a mocking, sour expression had as much rhythm in his body as Sarah had discovered in her own. Soon the other dancers drew away, as they had done at the village hop, content to watch and admire this undisputed superiority of interpretation of the mood of the music - and this time the applause was for both dancers. The music stopped. Sarah and the punk stood facing each other. The disc-jockey was making some facetious but appreciative remarks about their display but neither of them was listening.

"Wow!" said Sarah.

"Yers! Wow! Wot a serprise ..." he snarled.

"You dance very well." said Sarah.

A slow smoochy tune had begun. He pulled her roughly to him and began to sway with her.

"Yer not too bad yerself," he said. "For a country girl."

Sarah pulled away - her feet still moving - but she looked at him reproachfully.

"Why did you nearly knock me over?" she asked.

"Wiv me machine?" He laughed mockingly. "Or - arfter?"

"Well - b-both," stammered Sarah.

"Forget it!" he growled. "Let's just take it from 'ere."

There was no question of Sarah changing partners from that point. If any boy dared approach her the scowl on the punk's face soon scared him off. Besides which, it seemed to be a general agreement that two such super movers should stay together and provide a floor show from time to time. As for him, he offered no information about himself nor did he seem curious about Sarah's background. He did say, "Been in any good taxis lately?" but Sarah, so happy to be dancing, just laughed. Later he offered her a drink and as Helen and Marjory were near the bar she made an attempt to introduce him.

"Some one I met near home," she said.

"Yers," he said. "I'm workin' in that caff now matter of fact - sort 'o - managin' it, like."

"Sally," said Marjory. "We won't be able to stay too late, you know. We've got to organise a lift."

" 'sorl right," he said. "I'll run 'er 'ome. On me bike."

"Oh charming!" said Helen, jealousy written all over her face. "And where does that leave us?"

Marjory said spitefully, "We're all at school - private school - for young ladies!"

He was nonplussed.

"Me an' my mates 'is broad-minded!" he declared. "'Ere - Frank - Geoff - orl right fer takin' these birds 'ome - you'll piss yersells when I tell you where they live ...."

He swung Sarah to her feet.

"Time we wus dancin'" he said.

Sarah was fascinated by his crude words, his tough features, his lithe, muscular body. Their steps became increasingly intricate. They dominated a whole corner of the clubroom. Then, Astaire-style, the punk began jumping on and off chairs, pushing himself off the wall, never losing the beat. He lifted Sarah on to a table. The crowd roared encouragement and willing hands swept the surface clear of glasses and ashtrays. Her partner, pretending exhaustion, straddled a chair and clapped his accompaniment to her steps.

Jane, on the edge of the audience, was at first horrified to recognise Sarah and know how desolate Paula would be to see her precious daughter making an exhibition of herself in front of this raucous crowd. But then she was caught up in the frenzied enthusiasm of the onlookers for such an uninhibited yet marvellously- controlled performance from this amateur who, in another dimension would surely have been dancing on a real stage professionally. Reluctantly Jane slunk away, taking the ostrich's way out - what she could not see she could not be held responsible for.

CHAPTER SEVENTEEN

Somehow the motorcyclists managed to acquire enough crash helmets to accommodate their passengers. The drive back to the school was at once frightening and exhilarating to Sarah who took to pillion riding almost as passionately as she had taken to dancing. She loved the feel of the wind on her face, the thrill of leaning over as they swooped round bends, the human bodies becoming part of the beautifully-engineered machine. The Punk drove recklessly however and soon Sarah realised that the more she yelled in his ear that he should slow down, the faster he went. The intimacy of the journey, her arms clasped round his waist, her head resting on his broad back, made her wonder how he would behave when they reached their destination. Would she have to endure a repeat performance of the

Reg episode. Remembering the way they had danced together she admitted it might not be such an ordeal. For the first time she had an inkling of what attracted Helen to her 'rough customers'.

Reconciled to some sort of sexual encounter she was shocked when her escort did not switch off his engine as she dismounted in the gateway. They had arrived well ahead of the others - the Punk, being leader of the pack, had to be given his head on the road. Sarah unbuckled her helmet and handed it to him. He hooked it on to the bike, said, "See yer ..." and drove off into the night. Sarah was flabbergasted - and a little disappointed. Her body rebelled against this rejection. She ached to be back on the powerful machine, the engine throbbing beneath her, the boy in her embrace. She longed to be dancing opposite his lithe body - his indifference had done more towards kindling her desire for him than his previous brutality. She wanted him - fiercely.

The other bikers roared towards her, drooping forlornly in the gateway and, taking their cue from their leader, dismissed the other two girls in an equally abrupt fashion.

"Well!" gasped Helen. "Talk about losing my touch!"

"Hmmm," agreed Marjory, also non-plussed. "Still, I must say I enjoyed the ride. How was yours, Sal?"

Sarah was sure the question meant more than it seemed to. She shrugged, unwilling to admit to her aroused interest and subsequent disappointment.

"He's a super dancer," was all she could muster.

"You can say that again," agreed Helen. "And another triumph for our Sally, Queen of Jive, eh?"

"Come on," urged Marjory. "We're sailing close to the wind with Schreiber. We'd better play it cool from now on. I vote we put in some hard graft and give them all the shock of their lives. I'd like to do your portrait, Sal."

....

They began the next morning. To Sarah's relief Marjory did not seem to have missed her sketchbook. This portrait was to be the real thing, in oils and posed in the Academy Studio, the converted Orangery, a place little frequented by the other students though a handful had chosen Art as an optional extra on top of typing and other secretarial skills. As she sat as still as possible, hour after hour, Sarah reflected on recent events. She tried to sort out her feelings for the punk. She tried to conjure up a picture of Jeremy who had affected her deeply in a different way. She compared the two very different young men. It was weird how many men she had 'brushed up against' in this very short time. As far as her emotions were concerned Fred, Reg and the detestable Roger were non-starters, whatever she may have pretended at the time. Deep feelings had been aroused only by her brief encounter with Jeremy and her two short meetings with the punk. If only she could have discussed it all with someone. But her mother was out of the question, Carol was far away and she could not entirely trust Marjory and Helen. If only I could find out why neither of the chaps I was interested in stayed interested in me, she thought wistfully.

It was this wistful look that Marjory had caught so well, Sarah saw, when at last she was allowed to look at the painting. She gasped at the new evidence of Marjory's talent.

"Where did you learn to paint like that?" she asked.

"Never you mind!" snapped Marjory.

Then, more kindly she added, "Do you really like it?"

"She'd be an eejit if she didn't," said Helen who was half-heartedly working on a still-life at a nearby easel. "You've flattered her disgracefully."

"No ..." said Marjory, glancing from portrait to sitter and back again. "But I've only got part of her - and it seemed so urgent to capture it - probably 'cos my guilty conscience tells me I'm likely to destroy it - that lovely quality of - well - innocence."

Helen snorted her contempt of such a notion. Sarah looked round for a mirror. She found a rather dusty one in a cupboard and studied her reflection.

"Am I becoming dissipated?" she asked,

Marjory joined Helen in a derisive laugh

"Oh, Sal - you're only a beginner!" she said. "Oh - it's no good, you know. I can't keep up this goody-goody stuff. We'll have to break out again, girls. Work is all right for the day but night time is for fun. Besides," she added, wiping her brushes and tidying her box of paints, "I saw that Inspector chappie earlier, going into the Lion's den. He gives me the creeps. I don't want to hang around here, thinking about what might have happened to Gill ..."

"But what could have happened?" asked Sarah, who was getting frustrated that the others refused to speculate on the possible fate of the missing girl.

"What indeed!" said Helen gloomily. "Yes, Marge - you're right. Let's hitch again."

"I don't know about that," said Marjory.

"Oh, come on - he was harmless," said Helen, obviously referring to the lorry driver who had been so obliging.

"My God, Helen - he was decrepit!" said Marjory bitterly.

Helen shrugged.

"Makes a change," she said.

"You'd go for anything!" cried her friend and went out, slamming the door behind her.

Helen looked at Sarah.

"Poor Marge," she said. "I wish I could be what she wants for me - but I must ... while I can ...."

Her voice faded away and she stared ahead, lost in some private world Sarah felt totally incapable of entering.

....

By evening Marjory had calmed down. At supper she talked of spending the night in the Academy after all.

"Maybe I'll put a few finishing touches to the portrait," she said to Sarah. "If you don't mind, that is ..."

Sarah bit her lip. She could see Miss Schreiber at the High Table, looking down on her malevolently. She would have liked to get away.

"Where's Helen?" she asked.

"Gone up to get changed. She's promised to call in at the studio. Help me persuade her to stay in for once."

As they came within sight of the door of the studio they heard a suppressed shriek. They hurried in - to find Helen standing before the portrait, staring at it in horror. She turned, white-faced, as they entered.

"Look," she whispered.

Slashed across the painting were thick, ugly stripes of red paint, obliterating the face of Sarah entirely. Blobs of the same colour had been daubed over the torso as if to represent blood. Marjory moved closer to Helen.

"What for?" she asked in fury.

Helen looked at her, horrified.

"You don't think I did this, Marge?"

She collapsed into tears. Marjory put her arms round her.

"I'm sorry, Helen, so sorry. Forgive me - of course you wouldn't do - that."

She put the clinging girl from her.

"And see ..."

She snatched up a rag.

"I think I can get this muck off and touch it up - it'll be as good as new."

Sure enough, under her expert touch, the red paint which had been hastily selected from a tray of poster colours, came away from the surface of the nearly-dry oils.

"I'll work on it some more tomorrow," she said. "We will go out - because if I stay here, I might well ..."

She turned to Helen. "C'mon - what else did you see?"

"O'Grady," said Helen. "I didn't exactly see her come out of here but she was in the corridor just before I came in and she had a look of triumph on her face."

"Help me cart this canvas upstairs," said Marjory. "We'll lock it in my wardrobe. Then if you two will keep cave I'll sneak into Matron's office and telephone Doug."

....

Doug and Phil seemed to have simmered down, forgotten their humiliation. They were waiting in a fairly-decent car which Phil swore he had legitimately borrowed from a cousin.

"Why didn't you bring the cousin?" asked Helen. "Sally's free tonight."

"Because the cousin is forty and very married," said Phil.

He and Doug exchanged glances.

"We'll pick up somebody for Sally," said Doug, with some of his old mockery.

"How about driving to the coast?" suggested Marjory.

"Too cold for midnight bathing, isn't it?" asked Phil.

"No, stupid. I mean - let's go to Bridgethorpe."

1"Right oh," said Phil. "It's as good a place as any to start with."

Sarah felt a thrill of anticipation. She felt sure the punk would be there. She could already imagine the sensation of dancing with him.

Doug and Phil, however, had other plans. The fact that they arrived early before the dance had started played right into their hands. After a round of drinks - Sarah insisted on a small shandy and watched it being poured - Phil said they should move on somewhere more lively. Marjory and Helen put up no argument. But as she stood waiting while Phil unlocked the car she heard, with a quick gladdening of spirits, the roar of engines. She just had time to catch a glimpse of the punk before she was bundled into the back seat with Helen and Doug. Phil drove back inland - to her old home town - a place Sarah had never particularly liked. They drove very near to the avenue where she and Paula and the ineffectual Harold had passed many unsettled, bewildering years. Sarah was silent, not wishing to mention her connection with this place to the ill-assorted company. She did not want to hear Doug and Phil taunting her about its poshness whereas she was sure Helen would be unimpressed with its middle class ordinariness. As for Marjory - her reactions was an unknown quantity - Sarah found her impossible to categorise. But now they were in a very classy part and Marjory was sitting up and taking notice.

"Where on earth are we headed?" she asked Phil. "This doesn't look like your kind of scene .."

"Oh, I think it will amuse you," sniggered Doug.

They drew up outside an elegant hotel. Inside all was quiet dignity. As the door swung to behind them Sarah thought she heard motorcycles. But no - surely she must have been mistaken.

The head waiter came forward and a couple of minions took their coats.

"Have you booked a table - sir?" he asked.

"We're meeting somebody," growled Doug, obviously aware of his own shortcomings. "In the Flamingo Room."

The little man bowed them towards pink-carpeted stairs leading down to a room arranged, night-club style, with small candlelit tables set round a dance-floor. People sat eating and drinking, talking in well-bred, hushed voices with an occasional peal of horsey laughter. At one table sat a solitary figure - he rose as they approached. It was Reg.

"Oh no!" gasped Sarah.

"How could you?" she asked of Phil.

He guffawed and to Sarah consternation, Helen and Marjory also seemed to be enjoying the joke.

"Oh, Sal - your face!" chuckled Helen.

"Come on, Sal - it's quite a funny trick - for Phil's infantile mind," said Marjory. "After all - you did make fools of them ..."

She moved close to Sarah and whispered.

"Play along, Sal, it's the only way with these eejits - I'll get you out of it later."

Sarah was not inclined to trust her - but then she recalled the sensitivity which had gone into the painting of her portrait - there must be a core of goodness in this girl. She tried to brave it out. She took her cue from Helen who had stepped forward and was speaking with an elegant drawl.

"Why, Reg - long time no see!" she said, holding out her hand. "Isn't this naice?"

Helen added to the fun.

"Do you come here often?" she asked, looking round disdainfully at the sleepy clientele. "Or only in the hibernating season?"

Reg pulled out a chair for Sarah but his grin was vicious.

"Hello, Teaser," he snarled. "I've a drink all ready for you. I hear you've been practising."

Sarah took the glass and defiantly gulped it down. Whisky! Ugh!

"Not bad!" she said, forcing herself to smile. "But could I have some - er - ginger in it?"

Phil and Doug sniggered.

"Whatever Madam wants," sneered Reg, summoning the waiter. "And afterwards - perhaps Madam would do me the honour of dancing - I hear you've been practising that too - and other things."

Sarah danced with Reg and found it extremely unpleasant to partner such a clumsy mover. She found drinking preferable - but tried to be prudent in memory of the last time she had indulged. As she sat sipping from her glass, amply topped up with a mixer and trying to avoid Reg's eyes staring lecherously at her, she felt a touch on her shoulder. She saw Marjory and Helen look up in surprise. Phil and Doug cowered. Without turning she knew it was the punk.

"C'mon!" he said.

Reg stood up, the veins in his neck standing out with anger. The manager appeared by their table.

"Er - ladies and gentlemen, the orchestra is leaving. There will be no more dancing tonight. Perhaps you also would like to leave."

"No dancing!" snarled the punk. He turned threateningly to the little man. "'Oo ses so?"

Sarah felt reckless again. Through a slight haze she was aware that the room, never brimming with people, was rapidly emptying. The diners were threading their way between tables, pointedly not looking in the direction of the fracas, the musicians were packing up their instruments. Reg took her arm. Quick as a flash the punk snatched up the empty ginger cordial bottle and smashed it on the edge of the table. Reg let go of Sarah and did the same with a tonic bottle. The manager turned appealingly to Sarah who had risen unsteadily to place herself between the two angry youths, brandishing their ugly weapons.

"Please, Miss - my licence - " he pleaded.

There was a clatter as one of the band dropped his cymbals. This tiny snatch of musical sound sparked off an idea in Sarah's dimmed consciousness. All she had wanted this evening was to dance. Hysteria took over. She pushed at the shoulder of the little man in his ridiculous tailcoat, tossed back her hair and laughed. The punk and

Reg, whether in amazement or because both were innate cowards, lost interest in their fight and turned to stare at Sarah. She was swinging the little fellow round and round across the dance floor, chanting, "Dance, dance, I must dance."

He broke away and hurried to the telephone. From the archway leading to the bar stepped a tall figure.

"Come with me, Sarah," he said.

Unbelieving, Sarah stared at him.

"Uncle George!" she gasped.

CHAPTER EIGHTEEN

George led Sarah out of the bar and into the lift. He glanced round and was relieved to see that no-one appeared to have noticed them leave. The lights in the Flamingo Room had been dimmed and there were sounds of confusion as people hurried away, not anxious to get involved in any trouble. George pressed the button and the doors slid across. He leaned on the mirrored wall and regarded his niece. Now that he had recovered from the first shock of seeing Sarah in a new light he noticed how attractive she had become. Her mane of hair half-covered her pretty features as she hung her head in shame. Uncle George! It was almost as if her father had stepped out of the grave and come back to save her in her hour of need.

"Sarah!" remarked George huskily.

"Oh, Uncle George - forgive me," she said and flung herself into his arms.

George reeled under the feel of her lissom young body pressed up against him. He put an arm round her and, with his other hand, loosened his collar.

"Wh-what are you doing here?" he asked, pulling her closer, relishing her warm sweetness.

"Oh - that college - it's so nasty!" she cried, aware of how impossible she would find it to explain to someone she had not seen for months - years even. She began to cry. George patted her head. The lift stopped.

"Never mind, now," he soothed. "Come along with Uncle George. I'll look after you."

Sarah nestled into his shoulder as they walked along the carpeted corridor. He fumbled to open the door without letting go of her but once inside Sarah broke away and began to explore the room curiously.

"I've never been in a such a grand hotel room before," she said, brighter now. "Why - it's a suite!" she discovered.

George felt a twinge of misgivings at her childish enthusiasm. She was, of course, still very young.

"Have you seen Mother lately?"

George's guilt vanished. He was still smarting from Paula's rejection of him. And now here was her daughter - his for the asking if he played his cards right. He turned on the radio and tuned in to some soft music.

"Let's have a drink," he suggested.

"To calm our nerves," he added as Sarah looked up in surprise from studying the hotel brochure.

"I don't drink much, really," said Sarah. "And - please don't tell Mother what you saw down there - she's a lot of troubles just now ..."

"Oh really?" said George indifferently.

He took a gulp of his drink and handed the glass to Sarah.

"Come on, share with your old uncle," he coaxed.

He took off his tie. Sarah tasted the drink.

"I really don't like whisky at all," she said.

George dimmed the lights.

"Never mind - come and dance with your old uncle then."

She shook her head, picked up a magazine. George pulled her to her feet.

"You seemed to be doing plenty of dancing down there!" he said roughly.

Then the feel of her silky skin was too much for him. He slid down on his knees, grasping her waist and kissing her firm young belly.

Sarah was horrified. But some instinct told her that she was in an impossible situation. She must play it cool - as Marjory would have said. She put a hand on George's thinning hair.

"Darling ..." she whispered.

George looked up into her face, gratified by the belief that he had aroused her.

"Sweetheart?"

"I must - go to the bathroom," she said, resisting the impulse to overact by winking knowingly.

Instead she stared at him as open-eyed as possible whilst inside she wanted to laugh and to cry at the same time. George lumbered to his feet. He opened the door to the bedroom and waved to a door on the further side.

"Through there," he said and went contentedly back to the drinks tray to ply himself with alcohol while he waited.

Sarah spotted the telephone on the bedside table. She went into the bathroom and flushed the toilet. She turned on both taps at the basin full blast. Then she crept back and dialled Fred's number.

....

Amazingly, George suspected nothing. Sarah went back into his sitting room.

"Boy, am I tired," she drawled. "I'll need a few stiff ones to keep me awake."

Delighted, George poured her a drink. He sat down beside her on the low sofa.

"Drink this, dearest," he said, " and then we'll - ahem - lie down together and rest."

Sarah wondered desperately how long she could fob him off. He was snuggling up to her already, resting his head on her shoulder. Then he put down his glass and began to stroke her knee, gradually rucking up the skirt of her dress. Sarah bent forward and picked up his glass. She offered him a sip, followed it with a kiss. George took to the game gladly. Sip after sip followed by kisses from those luscious young lips - and there was all the time in the world. He allowed Sarah to refill his glass. But finally this drink, too, was finished. Sarah was on the verge of panic.

George lumbered to his feet, turned to face her and fell down between sofa and table - dead drunk. Sarah ran to the window and looked down into the forecourt. There were no motorcycles, Phil's car had gone - but nor was there a sign of Fred's taxi. She remembered that she had had no time to mention the room number during the hasty conversation. She crept across the room, opened the door softly and went down the stairs. She said a silent prayer that Fred was not already in the lift or prowling about the corridors. But as she entered the foyer he was just coming in through the main door. He looked concerned - not angry but not too friendly either. "Sarah!" he admonished her.

The night porter looked up, astonished.

"Again!" said Fred severely.

The porter glanced outside to ensure that it was a taxi this forthright young man had driven into the forecourt. Then the squeak of the lift doors drew their attention. A dishevelled and furious George staggered out and approached Sarah menacingly.

"My father's brother!" announced Sarah - she had only given Fred the bare outlines of her difficulty over the phone.

The porter's spectacles slid off his nose as he jumped to his feet. Seeing more trouble brewing and already shocked at the implications of the situation, Fred decided that this was not the place to thrash matters out. He pushed Sarah into the revolving doors and followed her out. George, gasping and choking with rage and frustration, followed. Fred opened the back door of the taxi for Sarah and with amazingly quick reflexes, closed it on her and opened the front passenger door so abruptly that George was inside before he realised what was happening. Fred raced round to his side, jumped in and drove off.

"What the ..." spluttered George.

"Uncle George," said Sarah, calm now that she was under Fred's protection, "this is a friend of mine - and of my mother's."

Fred glanced round at her sharply but was soon convinced that what she had said did not imply that she had guessed at his relationship with Paula. She was simply calling this George fellow's bluff.

"I'm going to ask Fred not to say anything to Mother - about this evening," the girl went on. "That is - if you promise to behave. Fred will drive me back to college, then he'll take you back to the hotel - and I hope you will pay him well."

George nearly exploded. To be thus defeated by two Hanley women.

In the gateway of the Academy, Fred stepped out to have a word with Sarah.

"Are you sure you wouldn't rather come - er - go home?" he asked, looking at the distant facade of the school.

"Is Mother at the cottage?" asked Sarah.

"Yes - and your relative, Mary. If you are in trouble, Sarah - wouldn't you be better off with your mother?"

"She hasn't been in touch for days!" snapped Sarah bitterly. "I'm obviously not wanted. No, Fred, I'll be all right."

And she dashed off towards the gloomy building.

Fred felt very uneasy at leaving her. Thoroughly honest and straightforward himself, he had had his fill of other people's complicated machinations. He sighed and got back in the taxi. Not a word was spoken on the return journey. George got out in front of the hotel and contemptuously held out a ten pound note. As the cab drew away, George took out of his pocket the photograph he had found on the shelf under the dashboard. Fred's one indulgence in the face of his vow of secrecy was a small passport snapshot he had thought safely hidden from the eyes of the world. George smiled spitefully to himself as he entered his room. He resolved to pay a visit to his sister-in-law first thing in the morning.

....

Mary pottered round the cottage garden. She loved it, even in its winter sparseness. Having never owned a garden, she revelled now in all the little regular chores like deadheading and constant tidying.

She was much more painstaking than she had ever been with housework - though she insisted on doing more than her share of that for Paula too.

"This little place'll be a doddle to keep nice," she said. "And meself - I like it better than that there town 'ouse you 'ad."

Paula smiled, remembering how Mary had constantly professed undying admiration of the other house. But she could see her point. This trim little cottage bridged the gap between Mary's poor little terraced hovel and Paula's previous grand abode - also part of a terrace, funnily enough. They met here, the two women, on neutral ground. They were at last able to be friends.

Mary carried some old flower pots into the barn where she had spotted a sort of work bench. She stooped to stow them away on the lower shelf - and was surprised to see a number-plate lying there. It was buckled and Mary remembered the young cabdriver talking about it when he'd called yesterday to see if she were settling in all right. A pleasant young fellow, she had decided, and so considerate to be concerned for her - a complete stranger. Yes - he'd mentioned having a slight argument with a lorry - nothing serious but he'd need to get a new number plate. Mary straightened with a jerk. A flash of insight told her exactly why Fred had been so anxious to call here and why bits of his vehicle were in the outhouse. He was used to calling and parking the cab. Why - he was Paula's fancy man.

Mary was slowly digesting this when she heard a car. She hurried in through the back door, not altogether keen to meet Fred so soon after putting two and two together. But peering through the front room curtains she observed that it was not Fred striding up the path - it was - Mary felt faint. It couldn't be Paula's Harold, back from the dead. But no, of course, it was George, Harold's brother George. She opened the door.

"George Hanley," she said. "I haven't seen you for years."

George looked at her blankly.

"Mary!" she said. "I'm Paula's cousin-in-law Mary."

"Oh yes," said George without interest. "Is Paula in?"

"No," said Mary, hurt at his brusque manner.

People had been treating her so kindly lately - but then, of course, George wouldn't know.

"My Jack - Paula's real cousin, he was, you remember - he died," she explained.

George felt his patience cracking.

What was the old fool babbling about? And what the devil was she

holding? My God, a number plate. That young upstart's number

plate.

He snatched it from her.

"Where is that fortune-hunter?" he demanded.

Mary stared at him, stricken. He thrust his hand in his pocket and

brought out the photograph. He waved it in her face.

"Don't try to cover up for them - a regular little brothel you're

keeping here," he said, looking round as though he expected Fred

and Paula to come out of hiding any moment. "I know what's going

on ..."

"Oh you do, do you?" asked Mary.

She pulled herself together. This had decided her. She was firmly on

the side of the lovers.

"And just what has it got to do with you?" she continued, self-pity

forgotten in her indignant defence of Paula and Fred - some of the

old vivacious, vulgar Mary revived.

"Why don't you just go right back wherever you came from?" she

spat out at him. "We don't need you here. You're as bad as all the

Hanley men - you 'aven't got what it takes an' you can't bear anybody else to 'ave it. Well - for your information, Paula and Fred'll be gettin' wed soon - you just keep away."

George was bowled over. He backed off, unsure what to do next. He looked around in dismay, then flung down the snapshot, steamed off up the path and drove off. Mary picked up the photograph and took it upstairs. She put it in a drawer in Sarah's room which Paula had gladly given over for the time being to her friend.

CHAPTER NINETEEN

Mary was not the only person in the village who had accurately guessed Paula's secret. Miss Isobel, too, had kept her eyes and ears open and was not the least shocked by her conclusions. She was so gratified to see the happiness which glowed on Paula's face. Neither the discrepancy in age nor any difference in the couple's backgrounds worried her one jot.

"There's love in the air," she told Fanny as they set off for the church where brasses waited to be polished and vases seemed constantly in need of replenishment.

"It's not confined to Spring," she added mischievously as Cyril approached, a remarkable coincidence of timing which happened so regularly as to be quite transparent. Fanny understood perfectly the double meaning behind her sister's words but chose, as usual, to ignore this reference to romance in the Autumn of her life.

"Good morning, Cyril," said Isobel gaily.

Then, as she caught a glimpse of Fred's taxi rounding Elm tree Corner she said, "You go on ahead, Cyril, Fanny - there's someone I must see..."

Fanny and Cyril put up no argument. They disappeared inside the porch.

Isobel stepped out from the shelter of the lych gate, almost into the path of the taxi. Fred braked hard and shook his head good-naturedly at Isobel.

"Now, Miss Willard," he gently admonished. "You mustn't step out into the road like that."

"Sorry, Fred," said Isobel. "But as a matter of fact, I'm glad to have - ahem - run into you like this."

Fred gave a wry smile at her wit.

"It's about Paula," said Isobel, watching his face.

"Mrs Hanley's not in any trouble, I hope?" he said quickly.

"Well, I'm not sure - the poor dear's not in the best of financial circumstances, as you may know."

Fred looked uncomfortable. What was the old biddy hinting at, he wondered. Surely she was not trying to warn him off from sponging on Paula.

"She's taken this cousin of hers under her wing," went on Isobel, pretending to be oblivious of Fred's frown. "And now she's told me she's thinking of cancelling Sarah's skiing holiday - she was to travel to Switzerland with my sister and I, you know - so that she can send Mary off on a little holiday instead."

"I see ..." said Fred.

He did not relish the prospect of Sarah taking Mary's place at the cottage. He had already sensed sympathy for himself in the widow - he had been considering suggesting to Paula that they take Mary into their confidence - if not the whole world, he ached to add but knew that the time was not yet ripe for that.

"You seem to know Mrs Hanley and Sarah quite well, Fred," said Isobel. "And believe me - that's no-one's business but your own."

As Fred stared at her, unsure how to reply to this bold statement, Isobel continued.

"I'd like your advice. I feel Paula would hate the thought of accepting charity but my sister and I are comfortably off. It would give us such pleasure to cover Sarah's expenses - what do you think?"

"I think you are a warm-hearted woman, Miss Willard," said Fred. "But I'm inclined to think you are right about Pau - er - about Mrs Hanley's reaction. She would see it as a handout, probably - but on the other hand - Sarah does need to get away from that place."

Isobel looked at him curiously and he was aware he had said more than he meant to. But he was genuinely concerned about young Sarah - not just because she was Paula's daughter. He had been racking his brains on how to handle things - he decided now that the stakes were too high - he must get help - and who better than Isobel Willard?

"I've had to pull Sarah out of some bad situations," he said in a low voice. "She's been keeping bad company. That college doesn't seem to be looking out for the girls at all. Even without what's been in the papers, I've no confidence in the place. There's something - I can't quite put my finger on it - things are not above board ..."

He gave Isobel a brief account of Sarah's scrapes and his own part in them. He did not mention George. Isobel listened, her face growing more and more angry.

"That cursed Fernleigh!" she muttered when he had finished. "That settles it. I'll see Paula right away. Thank you, Fred - and ... " she put a hand on his arm as it lay along the sill of the car window, "be good to her, won't you?"

Fred understood. He put his large hand over her delicate one.

"It's my only wish," he said. "To make her happy."

As Fred drove off and Isobel turned back into the churchyard, they both had tears in their eyes.

....

Miss Schreiber stood by the window of her office. She weighed up the advantages and disadvantages of her position. She took into account the recent unwelcome publicity caused by Gill Porter's disappearance. She balanced it against the phone-call she had just received from George Hanley. She thought long and hard. Then she went to the door. Seeing a student lurking about, waiting for the lunch bell, she called out.

"Find Sarah Hanley, tell her I want to see her at once."

The startled girl hastened off with the message. In less than five minutes, Sarah was facing Miss Schreiber across her huge desk.

"I'd like you to pack your belongings," said the headmistress, and her face showed neither anger nor triumph. It was as blank as she could make it.

"I am about to telephone the Governors to inform them that I have regretfully decided to expel you from Fernleigh."

"Wh-what?" stammered Sarah.

"I have just received a distressing telephone call from your uncle," said Miss Schreiber. "He informs me that he recently found you - OUT OF BOUNDS - in a BAR, behaving disgracefully. He has left it to my discretion - and I have decided I must telephone your mother and inform her of your reprehensible BEHAVIOUR."

"Why didn't he tell Mother?" Sarah burst out. "Have you thought of that - you've only heard his side of the story."

"The fact remains," said Miss Schreiber with ice-cold calm, "you have broken the COLLEGE RULES - can you deny that?"

"The college rules," said Sarah recklessly. "How can a college like this have rules?"

"What exactly do you mean by that?"

Schreiber glared at Sarah till she felt almost hypnotised into believing that the confrontation in her bedroom had taken place only in her imagination.

"Well - er - Gill - she ran away ..." gulped Sarah.

"Yes! And I have been very disturbed to learn of a certain an amount of CRUEL BULLYING amongst you girls."

"Amongst the girls!" gasped Sarah, incredulous.

Miss Schreiber looked grim. She picked up the telephone.

Sarah thought of Paula sitting snug and confident in the cottage. Of the shock and disgrace she would feel if she were asked to take her daughter out of the college. Her heart sank.

The Lion's too strong for me, she thought. I can't win.

Not yet sure of her intention, Sarah walked slowly round the desk till she was almost touching the teacher. She took the receiver out of her hand and slowly replaced it on the stand. Schreiber collapsed back on her chair, breathing heavily. She put up her hand as if to defend herself against the slight figure leaning towards her. Her tree trunk legs were spread apart, grossly. Her huge bosom heaved, her lips parted.

"Sarah ..." she pleaded.

There was a peremptory knock on the door and Miss O'Grady entered. A hiss of anger issued from her lips as she took in the scene. Then she spoke hurriedly.

"Isobel Willard is here to see you."

Schreiber sprang out of the chair but not before Isobel, following close on the heels of O'Grady, had seen enough to draw her own conclusions.

"Hello, Sarah," she said calmly. "Why don't you go upstairs and get your things?"

Bewildered at a second order to leave Fernleigh, but impressed by the new fire in Miss Willard's eyes, Sarah went out. She hardly noticed O'Grady still in the doorway but as the teacher made as if to follow the girl, Isobel called out.

"In here, Siobhaan - I want to talk to both of you."

As the door closed Sarah thought she heard Isobel saying something about getting away with it once too often - corruption - ruin her life like Fanny's.

Sarah could not quite grasp what was happening. Her mind was in a haze. But before she reached the stairs the doorbell rang. She went to open it automatically, moving zombie-like in her state of confusion - and admitted Inspector Bloom.

"I - I'm s-sorry, Miss Schreiber's got someone in there," stammered Sarah, shuddering as she had to voice the name of the Principal, now to be despised as a coward rather than feared as a bully.

"You all right, Miss?" asked the policeman, looking keenly at Sarah's white face.

The more he saw of this place, the more he thanked his lucky stars that he had a couple of sons - happily entrenched in the Comprehensive system. This privileged young girl - she looked ill and scared, under some terrible strain. What was it with this place, he wondered for the hundredth time since he had got involved in the case.

"What's going on?" he asked, leading her to a bench.

"N-nothing," stuttered Sarah. "My - aunt has just arrived - to take me away," she added, stabbing at the truth.

"Why's that then?" he asked.

"I've - there's trouble at home - a relation has died," said Sarah, relieved to not have to actually lie.

"Oh, I see," he said gruffly. "But - just before you rush off - is there anything more you would like to tell me about Miss - about Gill Porter?"

Sarah did not know why she should still feel this chill fear. Isobel offered refuge: it was clear she was on Sarah's side - and yet Sarah could not bring herself to voice her suspicions.

"Marjory and Helen," she said. "They know more about it."

"About what?" he asked. "Come on, Miss, I'm here to help."

"I know," said Sarah miserably. "And I'd like to help - truly I would - but I'm so confused ..."

The Inspector was moved: he assumed she meant that her emotions were in a tangle about the death in her family. Regretfully he let her go, noting down the names Marjory and Helen in his book. Soon after Sarah had gone upstairs the study door opened. All three women stared at the uniformed man waiting in the hall. Isobel stepped forward as though to speak to him but thought better of it. She turned instead to Siobhaan O'Grady, cringing behind her, "I'll go and give Sarah a hand," she said coldly. "I won't see you again."

She walked up the stairs having no difficulty finding her way.

Miss Schreiber had regained her composure.

"Can I help you, Inspector?" she asked. "Have you any news for us?"

"I'd like to make a few more enquiries," said Inspector Bloom. "I'll have to interview some of the girls again, I'm afraid."

He decided not to single out any names.

"I've already spoken to Miss Hanley."

He did not fail to notice the wary look which passed between the two teachers. His intuition about Sarah being at the hub of this business had been right then. He regretted letting her go without finding out more.

"Come into the study," said Miss Schreiber. "We'll draw up a list."

....

"May I say goodbye to my friends?" asked Sarah.

Isobel had just finished explaining whilst they packed that Paula had given her permission to fetch Sarah away.

"We're taking the holiday earlier than planned," she said, choosing her words with care so as not to alarm the terrified-looking child further. "Your mother has taken Mary to the coast - they'll be back to see us off. Meanwhile you can stay with Fanny and me. We've all your ski-ing stuff to get - we're so looking forward to it ..."

"Ah," said Sarah who had not taken in half of what Miss Willard had said. "Here's Marjory now. Hello, friend, meet Mother's friend ..."

Her voice faded away. When she had found Marjory's self-portrait in her sketch book and then been confronted with the man it so closely resembled she had wondered who else it reminded her of. Now she knew. For Isobel too had been stunned by the likeness of this girl to her dear Fanny. Marjory stared back as they both gazed at her. Who was this funny old duck holding Sal's suitcase, she wondered, and why was she looking at her as if she were a ghost?

"What gives?" she asked.

"I'm taking Sarah away," said Isobel.

She was clutching at the lace jabot she wore round her throat, her masterly self-assurance quite shattered for the moment.

"Sally - you must try to give up being rescued," chuckled Marjory. She and Helen had easily forgiven Sarah for deserting them for her Uncle George. The excitement and adventure of getting out of the hotel before the police arrived had made up for a certain envy of Sarah who seemed to have found the most thrilling finale to the outing. Of course they had teased and quizzed her when she finally climbed back into school - and Sarah had summoned up enough bravado to give the impression of having had yet another fascinating experience.

"Have you got Ginger Fred outside?" Marjory said mischievously to Isobel. "His taxi usually turns up on these occasions."

Isobel seemed to be having difficulty breathing.

"No!" she gasped. "No - Fred is - er - busy. Jeremy brought us."

Sarah's heart stood still. Jeremy was here - at the door, in his beloved vintage car.

"We must dash," she said to Marjory. "Give my love to Helen - take care of her - I'll write. Come on, Miss Isobel ..."

She snatched her bag and half-dragged Miss Willard down the stairs. She flung open the door - and there he was. Jeremy, brushed, groomed, handsome. And smiling warmly at her. He stepped forward and took her case.

"Hello again!" he said and Sarah thought she would melt under his welcome gaze.

CHAPTER TWENTY

The month that followed was all that Paula could have ever dreamed of for her daughter. For Sarah it was so idyllic as to be almost unreal after her time of torment. Content to have her life organised so pleasantly, she passively let it all happen. The brief time with her mother, checking her well-stocked trunks, gave her an inkling of a subtle change in Paula but her cushioned existence did not allow her to puzzle her head about it - any more than how the money had miraculously appeared to pay for all these new clothes and the holiday as well.

She took to Mary, too, but any twinge of curiosity as to her new status in their life was superficial. Remembering that Jane was her own age she held up one of her new outfits and mumbled something about how unfair it seemed that Jane should have to work in a holiday camp while she, Sarah, was to enjoy the luxury of going abroad - and ventured a hint of her concern that Paula could not really afford it. Mary scoffed it off -

"I expect your Uncle George has coughed up - and I should think so too - you being all the family he's got."

Sarah was totally unable to make sense of this so chose to let the matter drop.

The journey - the holiday - everything was wonderful - but seemed to pass in a dream. Jeremy was ever present, attentive and protective, whether teaching her how to cope on skis, ordering her dinner, dancing with her evening after star-studded evening. Isobel loomed large at the extremities of the day - tucking her up each night with a cup of hot chocolate - greeting her every morning with coffee and croissants. And gently persuading her to take some vicious green pills and swallow the thick white medicine prescribed by her own doctor to soothe Sarah's shattered nerves.

Then, one afternoon, it was as though a fog suddenly cleared in her mind. She was jolted into awareness by an urgent pricking at her senses. She felt the hard wooden settle beneath her, the warmth from the log-fire, the tasteful comfort of the chalet's living room. Someone had just been speaking - had they really been saying that this was the last day of the holiday.

Isobel, sitting opposite, was at once conscious of the girl's "return".

"My dear," she said, leaning across and patting Sarah's knee. "You look - all of a sudden - so much better."

"Ye - es," said Sarah, happily. "I do suddenly feel - wonderful. How very nice it is here ..."

Isobel let her be for a few minutes and watched as her eyes roved round the room, drinking in its charms as though seeing it properly for the first time. She wandered over to the picture window and looked out over the white landscape. Then she turned back.

"Miss Willard?" she ventured.

"Oh, Sarah, my dear - don't stop calling me Isobel now ..."

She came to her and put an arm round her thin shoulders.

Gently she said, "You have been quite - ill - my dear."

"Ill?"

"Yes - a kind of nervous breakdown. But the doctor said it would lift as suddenly as it came - and he was right. I'm so glad."

She led Sarah back to the fireside and poured her some tea. How good it tasted. Sarah reached for a pastry and munched it greedily. She looked up, embarrassed to find Jeremy staring at her as she licked sticky crumbs from her fingers.

"Oh - I'm sorry," she said to them both. "I just felt so very hungry - all of a sudden."

Jeremy laughed, delighted.

"I'm so glad!" he said and sat down on the rug at her feet with a familiarity that made Sarah's heart glow with pleasure: so her fantasy time with this suitor by her side had been for real.

"Where is Miss Fanny?" she asked after a few moments of companionable silence while Jeremy helped her finish off the goodies.

Isobel smiled contentedly.

"Off on her honeymoon - with Cyril," she said. "That's one of the reasons Jeremy kindly agreed to come with us, remember - he felt guilty for his uncle whisking our Fanny away - it was a quiet wedding, Sarah - and you were not well enough to attend - I'll show you the photographs later. But for now, I'll leave you young people if you don't mind. I've some last minute arrangements to make with my caretaker ..."

"Is the Willard family very rich?" asked Sarah when they were alone.

She felt she could ask Jeremy anything.

He turned and knelt in front of her.

"Aunt Fanny!" he chuckled. "I love calling her that - yes, they are quite well off. Better than me at the moment. I work with Father - we're solicitors, you remember - one day I shall be well set up."

Sarah looked down into his dear face. She did not need to wonder why he was explaining his affairs to her, what he was building up to.

"I was going to wait till this evening, my darling," he said. "And choose a romantic moment, after dinner, on the terrace of the hotel ballroom, perhaps, in the moonlight - but now I'm sure is the ideal moment after all."

He took both her hands in his.

"Sarah, my love - you will marry me, won't you - let me take care of you. I know you are very young but I can wait as long as you like - just give me hope."

Through Sarah's mind flashed instances of the time they had spent together - far away from the terrors of Fernleigh Academy - a tumble in the snow, both of them shaking themselves like puppy dogs, then Jeremy steadying her on her skis, looking at her with devotion - a troupe of boys and girls in national costume giving a display of traditional dances in the town square, she and Jeremy applauding loudly then looking into each other's eyes - the waiter leading them to a table, holding her chair, then Jeremy handing her an orchid corsage. All that had really happened. It was no dream.

"Yes, Jeremy," she whispered, suddenly shy.

He leaped to his feet, gave a boyish whoop of joy and then pulled her up and encircled her with his arms.

"Darling," he muttered into her hair. "I was so afraid that you'd been too - confused - to realise what was happening ..."

He hardly loosened his hold on her when Isobel reappeared, coughing apologetically.

"We're engaged, Isobel!" he cried. "Come and congratulate me!"

"My dears!" she said and hurried across to embrace them both.

....

Now that Sarah was making such an excellent recovery from her Anxiety State, as it had been officially labelled, it was thought that a job in an office would be good for her. Jeremy's father was glad to find a place for her, declaring in his blustery way that the old place could do with brightening up - much to the chagrin of his devoted, middle-aged secretary. Miss Barnes, however, soon took to Sarah and was pleased to show the quick-minded young girl the ropes. Besides, she was enjoying the ephemeral thrill of young Jeremy's romance, having watched him grow up, motherless, from the age of six. As soon as Sarah had realised that Mr Fox was a widower, and even more after she had met him and found him so attractive and charming, she had set her hopes on a relationship developing between him and Paula. He certainly went to a lot of trouble to introduce the Hanleys into his social circle but Paula, who at one time would have seized this chance eagerly, now made only the polite gestures that were incumbent on her as mother of the bride-to-be.

Standing under the cherry tree in Isobel's garden Sarah said to Jeremy, "Wouldn't it be wonderful - your father and my mother - a double wedding."

Jeremy kissed her.

"You can't do that," he warned. "Arrange other people's feelings. Just play it cool - remember I love you."

Nevertheless, Sarah could not resist hinting the same thing to Mary.

"No, oh no!" said Mary, too hastily.

"Why not?"

Sarah wondered if Mary were a little jealous.

"Your mother mun mek 'er own life," said Mary. "I wouldna say owt like that to 'er, Sarah."

Sarah felt ashamed of suspecting Mary's motives. She knew she put Paula's happiness before her own. She decided to take her advice. They were all getting on so well. Mary had taken over the running of the cottage. Paula tentatively suggested that she, herself, like Sarah, could now look for a job.

"No!" said Mary unexpectedly vehement.

"What?" said Paula?. "Why not?"

"I know it's all goin' well at the moment," said Mary. "But it is a bit of a squash 'ere - I'd like Sarah to have her own room back. And to 'ave some time alone with you. A daughter needs 'er mother just afore she gets wed. I don't want to be in the way o' that."

"Oh, Mary," protested Paula, but she had already realised that there was a lot of sense in what she had said. And she had been anxious to get round to talking to Sarah about Fred.

As though reading her mind Mary said, "Afterwards - until you and - until you decide what you are going to do ..."

Mary was referring to Fred's self-inflicted three month exile. Paula ached for the solid comfort of his nearness - even when he was only on the other side of the village she missed him dreadfully - but then he had been offered a driving job on a safari holiday in Africa. With the agreement of his partners who grieved for his restlessness yet still felt unwilling to pry into his affairs - he had accepted the job. He swore that the moment he got back he would force Paula to come to a decision about their future whether Sarah was totally recovered and settled or not.

"Afterwards," continued Mary now, "I'll come back to you for a while and I don't mind tellin' you that I 'ope it'll be to 'elp you get ready for your weddin'. But for the moment - I'm ready to go back to Jack's 'ouse an' pick up the threads - spend a bit o' time wi' our Jane, mebbee."

It was agreed. Sarah and Paula would quietly plan the wedding. Charles Fox and Jeremy would continue to escort them to functions to meet the people Sarah would be spending the rest of her life amongst. Isobel would play hostess to several of the pre-wedding family gatherings. Cyril and Fanny, contentedly established in the Vicarage, also joined gaily in the preparations.

A small spanner was thrown in the works when Charles was taken ill. He had a mild heart condition which flared up from time to time. This attack could not have been more ill-timed. There was important business in Scotland, needing immediate attention. Jeremy would have to go in his father's place.

Feeling lonely one evening when her mother had gone over to consult with Isobel over one of the thousand details connected with the wedding, Sarah wandered out to post a letter to Helen. She had already invited both her Fernleigh friends to the wedding and they had both accepted with genuine rejoicing in her happiness. They sent news of the Academy. The college was closed and rumours abounded. The strangest one was that Schreiber had supposedly gone off abroad somewhere with the owners of Fernleigh Grange. Sarah thought of the time she had seen the mysterious couple in their garden - and the odder occasion when she had seen the woman conspiring with the Lion in the pub. These monstrous people had long since ceased to haunt her dreams - the whole episode of her one term at the Academy seemed no more now, partly with the help of drugs and counselling, than a half-remembered nightmare. But now her attention was drawn to the cafe. She had not given a thought to that episode either - she never walked in this direction, having taken to cutting across the Village Green to get to the Willards or the village shops. But there he was now - the Punk. He was standing in the car park, by his motorcycle, staring across at her, expecting her to cross over to him. Sarah found herself inexplicably doing exactly that. She did not want to - her feet just seemed to move towards him of their own accord.

She stood by his bike as he straddled it, grinning at her.
"Wanna coffee?" he asked.
"No- thank you."

"Aw - c'mon. Long time no see. Come in and look wot I've done to the old place."

Maybe I should lay this one last ghost, thought Sarah, stepping over the thresh-hold, burningly aware that there was no likelihood of Fred appearing this time.

Inside all was garish and vulgar. Chrome stools at an orange counter. A jukebox dominating the scene. A crowd of young people who seemed vaguely familiar. The Punk selected a disc. A hit tune blared out. He faced Sarah and began to dance, Sarah felt herself lost - dragged back - and down - she gave in and began to move with the music.

CHAPTER TWENTY-ONE

Sarah hated the double life she was leading. She despised herself for deceiving Jeremy. Any comparison between him and Steve made her doubt her own sanity. How could she choose the brutish company of the Punk after having basked in the loving companionship of her fiancé? Maybe those words Anxiety State on the doctor's certificate are just another term for insanity, she told herself during a brief respite from dancing in the run-down flat where one of the motorcycle gang was giving yet another all-night party. She despised herself, too, for deceiving her mother. Paula, more relaxed now, had made one or two attempts to confide her own hopes for the future. But now it was Sarah who shied away from such intimacy. She was afraid of giving herself away. She looked round Andy's home - no, that was not the word - home was somewhere like the bungalow Jeremy had bought for them. This - this was just a dump where Andy kept his few squalid possessions and invited his friends to drink and shout lewd jokes at each other. It filled her with self-disgust, her being here. The chair she was sitting on was grubby and sticky - no attempt had ever been made to clean or decorate. She scorned herself too for betraying the trust of Isobel Willard. She knew that Isobel was the only one of her immediate circle who was fully aware of the evil influence of Fernleigh. She had had to fight down unpleasant personal memories in order to come to Sarah's rescue there. She had shown herself a true friend, despite the difference in their ages. She had also shown great interest in Marjory.

"I hope I can have a long chat with your friend at the wedding,"
she'd said, after questioning Sarah about Marjory's background.
The wedding! Sarah leaned over the side of the threadbare armchair
and groped for her glass. It was Coca-Cola - she was determined to
at least avoid the trap of strong drink - it was bad enough that she
could not conquer her craving for bad company. Anyway - this
crowd could hardly afford whisky. She looked through the open door
to the squalid kitchen where a crate of beer had been dumped on the
filthy draining board. It was hypocritical of her to sneer at them, she
realised, but they really were so crude - so lacking in ambition.
Steve, the punk, seemed the only one to have a regular job and now
he had told her he was considering "chucking it all in and movin'
dahn to the smoke". He had announced this intention casually - no
suggestion of wanting her to go with him - or any regret at leaving
her.

I hate him, she told herself. I must be more like Helen than I
admitted - needing a bit of rough - no, it's not him, it's me I hate.
But he was approaching her now, drinking from a can and she knew
that even though he hadn't the grace to even ask her nicely, she
would not refuse to dance with him.

....

Marjory turned up at the office one lunch time.

"I was in the area," she explained. "Look, love, I might not be able to make it to the wedding after all - can you come out to lunch?"

They sat in a coffee bar and Marjory tried to answer Sarah's tirade of questions.

"There was some ghastly racket going on next door at Fernleigh Court," she said. "Schreiber and - the woman there - were running it. A sort of private hospital for girls of good families who were - in trouble, as old-fashioned folk like your Miss Willard would call it - up the spout they say nowadays. Some of the - er - patients - were foreigners - and there was a very lucrative Private Adoption scheme for the babies."

Sarah thought of the beautiful woman in the garden. She had certainly not looked like a criminal. And as for her companion ...

"The man over there ..." she began.

Marjory nodded. "Yes - to whom you very kindly gave my drawings ..."

"No!" gasped Sarah. "It wasn't like that."

Marjory put her hand over Sarah's trembling one.

"I know - eejit - but you could have told me. You see, I knew he was staying there. The woman you saw was married to his brother. I'd talked to him in the pub and I knew him - before. As it is, it's all turned out all right."

She looked into Sarah's eyes.

"He's my father, you see."

Sarah's hand was still trembling as she stirred her cappuccino.

"Oh, Marjory, I'm so sorry."

"For what?" laughed Marjory. "We're together now. He's taking me to Italy. He likes my work and I like his. He's quite famous. And he wants to get away from the scandal his sister-in-law was involved in. He was never mixed up in their rackets! Except - well, it's a long story and even I don't know all the details yet. He lost my mother because of that place. Her family turned her against him and allowed me to be adopted. He hasn't talked about her a lot and apparently she's married someone else now. But he and I will be O.K. together, Sarah. I've always been so - lost, you see. And he's made me see it wasn't so bad being brought up by my adopted family. We'll

probably see his brother out there - they're twins and ... "

She stopped abruptly as though she had said more than she intended.

"Will you see Carol, then?" asked Sarah eagerly.

Marjory looked down at her plate.

"Sarah ..." she began.

Then she seemed to change her mind. She looked up and spoke

brightly.

"Hey - you haven't asked about old Helen!"

Before Sarah could object to her changing the subject she went on.

"She'll be coming to your wedding - with her fiancé, all official, a

diamond as big as a duck egg - the Honourable Albert, no less."

"Her boy-next-door ...?" ventured Sarah.

"That's right. And now that I've handed her over, so to speak, I'm just

not going to worry about her any more - though I'm sure poor Bertie

is taking on a handful."

There was a silence between the two girls.

"I'll walk you back to that funny old office," offered Marjory at last.

"Honestly, Sal - it's straight out of Dickens - this whole town too -

not enough life for me - I can't wait to see Rome."

"I -I've been seeing Steve," Sarah confessed as they strolled through the little park which was the hub of the sleepy little town which Sarah now saw through Marjory's eyes as rather dull. She elaborated, with a challenge in her voice, as though refusing to be classified with the town as old-fashioned, predictable.

"You know - the punk!"

"Eejit - super eejit!" said Marjory, stopped in her tracks by this unwelcome news. "Oh don't go and mess things up, Sarah."

"I can't help it."

Marjory put a hand on her shoulder and looked her rather cruelly straight in the eye.

"You wanted to know about Carol," she said. "Carol, your idol, the Unconventional One with a Wild Side like our Helen's - like me - perhaps like you, Sal, but I don't think so, not really. Carol never got to Paris. She spent less than a month with my father's brother and never very far from Fernleigh. Then he ducked the notoriety - like my father ducked acknowledgement of me for so long - they're both weak. Now Carol is a "case" on the police records - just like Gillian. She, too, disappeared without trace. And in my opinion we'll never know what happened to either of them - but you can bet it was not a happy ending. And that's what you can have, Sarah, and what I wish you - a happy ending."

Suddenly she put both arms round Sarah, hugged her and kissed her on the cheek, wetting Sarah's face with her tears. Then she hurried away, leaving Sarah feeling dizzy and bewildered.

CHAPTER TWENTY-TWO

Paula stared out of the window of her daughter's bedroom. The garden was in darkness. She could just make out the outlines of the barn.

"Have you loved anyone else?" whispered Sarah, still lying in the bed, the quilt up to her chin.

Mother and daughter knew that this question had been hovering between them for a long time.

Paula came close to the bed and knelt so that her face was close to Sarah's. She looked into her daughter's eyes. Part of her mind registered that the girl had been wearing eye-shadow which had been hastily removed. The cover slipped away and she saw that her child was half-dressed in her oldest clothes. Paula shivered. Instantly the girl pulled the quilt across so that it covered them both. Paula was crying silently, in response to the tears she had seen in Sarah's eyes.

"You don't love Jeremy?" she asked. "You've met someone else? Oh, my darling child, I'm so sorry - so sorry - forgive me. I'll help you - I'll tell Jeremy and his father - nothing else matters - you must choose love."

They clung to each other as if trying to make up for all the years of non communication, distance, waste.

Sarah remembered with another part of her mind Jeremy lifting a strand of her hair and holding it against his face. In the same instant she recalled Steve, roughly grabbing a handful of her tousled tresses, jerking back her head, kissing her hard and then speaking in his guttural voice.

"For this you'll ride with me - 'elmet or no 'elmet, eh, sugar?"

In her mind's eye she tried to imagine introducing him to her mother - his rudeness, her mother's horror. And she remembered her own feeling of repulsion earlier as he held her prisoner by his bike - his arrogance, his unpleasing odour, his viciousness. And his total lack of concern for her safety, riding pillion, head unprotected. She didn't hate him. She just wanted to be as far away from him as possible - to be rid of him for ever. She had torn herself from his grip and raced back to the cottage. Dumbfounded, he followed her on the motorcycle for a few metres, revving the engine loudly, quite unconcerned about the noise and nuisance he was creating. Then, turning the bike with a horrible screech of tyres, he roared off after his friends.

Sarah had let herself in, scrubbed at her face with the corner of a wetted towel and, hearing her mother stirring, had jumped into bed, pulling up the covers to hide her clothes.

Now she gently pulled her mother into bed beside her, abandoning all pretence of being in her nightie. She put her arms round her mother.

"Hush," she said. "You've got it all wrong, Mummy. I love Jeremy - in spite of his suitability."

She sat up and hugged her knees.

" I love his gentleness - his gentlemanliness. I shall marry him in the morning and I shall live happily ever after and I'll always be grateful to you for bringing me up, for preparing me for a good marriage, for educing me better than any Fernleigh Academy could do. This other boy, you see, I had to find out for myself ..."

It was Paula's turn to hush Sarah. She propped herself more comfortably against the pillows.

"You can tell me about him some other time if you still want to," she said.

"But now there's something I've been needing to tell you - about myself."

****

****

Sarah, a woman now, and passionately happy in her fulfilment, aware of shades and layers of emotion she could never have imagined or been taught, lay in her husband's arms and spared a thought for her mother.

****

****

Paula sat up late, by the fire, in the small living room of the cottage from which she had seen her daughter depart, a vision of loveliness in her wedding outfit. She recalled the service conducted by their friend Cyril, proudly watched by his wife Fanny. She remembered Isobel pressing her arm to lend her strength at the most moving part of the Vows. The reception, too, was a joy to recall, going off without a hitch, Jeremy's father, in much better health, revelling in the toasts. Jane and Mary had seemed to get on remarkably well with Sarah's friend Helen and her charming husband-to-be. They seemed to be sharing a lot of jokes - it was good to hear Mary laughing again. And Helen had been at one moment deep in conversation with Isobel - they seemed to be exchanging addresses, arranging something - Paula caught the words Marjory and Fanny but could not make head nor tale of it amongst the general happy sounds of laughter and congratulations.

But now she could hear an even more welcome sound as the car she had been waiting for drove down the lane and round to the barn. She went to the back door and stood waiting for the man she loved.

*** END ***

Fiction by *Sophie Meredith*

WITH MEN FOR PIECES

LESSONS

THE SPLENDOUR FALLS

OTHER PEOPLE'S GHOSTS

———————————

Short Stories available as Kindle Singles

ABUSE

A GIFT FROM GRAN

AIRPORT ADVENTURE

A PROSPECT OF RAINBOWS

AUTUMN

CAREER GIRL

GREAT AUNT HARRIET

MAGIC HOT WATER BOTTLE

SMALL CHANGES

SUMMER CHILD

THE GRASS IS GREENER

THE PLANTATION

VELVET'S CHOICE

For children

MIKE DOTT, MOUSE DETECTIVE

———

Essays by Sophie Meredith available on Amazon

LIES

CALLED OUT OF RETIREMENT

WHO WILL CATCH ME IF I FALL?

A DAY IN MARSEILLE WITH BOUILLABAISSE

Printed in Poland
by Amazon Fulfillment
Poland Sp. z o.o., Wrocław